C000148117

Ascension

Ascension

C.J.M. NAYLOR

Copyright © 2020 by C.J.M. Naylor

All rights reserved. No part of this publication may be reproduced, distributed, or transmitted in any form or by any means, including photocopying, recording, or other electronic or mechanical methods, without the prior written permission of the publisher, except in the case of brief quotations embodied in critical reviews and certain other noncommercial uses permitted by copyright law. For permission requests, write to the publisher, addressed "Attention: Permissions Coordinator," at the address below.

C.J.M. Naylor
cjmnaylor@gmail.com

Cover Design by Alexander von Ness

Printed in the United States of America

First Edition

For all those that have inspired me to keep going. This one's for you.

And also for my dog, Scout, because I love her.

PROLOGUE

11, 700 Years Ago

Waves crashed against the jagged rocks of the cliff. The sky was an orange, red color as the sun slowly crept beneath the horizon. Lucinda stood watching all of it, at the edge of the cliff, her favorite place to be. Her place to escape ever since her people had settled here. She enjoyed the breathtaking view, the breeze brushing against her cheeks, the peacefulness of it all.

A hand touched her shoulder and she turned to find her mother had crept up behind her.

"I didn't mean to scare you," she said.

"You didn't," Lucinda said, turning back to look at the view. "Isn't it beautiful?"

"Very much so."

They were looking out at the Dingle Peninsula. They hadn't been there for very long, but Lucinda was glad that they had come. It was one of the more beautiful places that they had settled.

She looked back at her mother. "I hope we are going to stay here."

Her mother smiled and kissed her forehead. "I'm confident we will. Come back to the hut soon."

Lucinda nodded and her mother walked away. She turned back to look at the view once more and something caught her eye down by the water. There was a woman she hadn't seen before. An old woman. She too was standing and looking out at the sea. Curiosity got the best of Lucinda and she found herself making her way down the cliffs. As she approached the woman, she saw she was holding a staff in one hand. She was barefoot and wore a robe that billowed around her in the wind.

And she was looking directly at Lucinda.

Closer up, the woman was even older than Lucinda first thought. Her skin was frail, almost as thin as paper. What was left of her hair blew in the wind and around her face.

"Who are you?" Lucinda asked.

The old woman smiled. "I am the Timekeeper." She gestured toward the side of the cliff. "Come."

Slowly, the old woman began to move toward the side of the cliff and waved her staff in the air. An entrance appeared out of nowhere. Lucinda stood there, completely frozen. What was happening? How had this woman done this? The woman turned around and gestured again for Lucinda to follow her. Lucinda took a deep breath and obeyed.

As soon as Lucinda and the old woman entered into the cliff, the entrance closed up. For a brief moment, she worried that the old woman was tricking her and that she would be trapped, but the worry went away. She felt safe with this woman. As soon as the cave went dark, fire lit in torches lined along the walls. Lucinda looked ahead of her and saw stairs that descended. She followed the old woman down.

Lucinda noticed the markings along the walls as she walked. They were similar to markings that her people had made on walls of caves that they had stayed in at one point in time.

The old woman led her deeper and deeper into the cave down to a circular room with archways where Lucinda noticed many more passageways leading off into different directions. She wondered where each of them went. In the middle of the circular room stood an altar.

The old woman led Lucinda down one of the passageways, past the altar, and they descended further and further down until they were at the edge of a large body of water. It was almost like a small ocean inside the cave. The old woman, or the Timekeeper as she had called herself, fell to her knees, dropping her staff beside her. She gestured out toward the water.

"This is Time," she said. "There has always been a Timekeeper. An individual that oversees the events of the world and records them so that Time can keep going. When Time began, there was a Timekeeper, and when Time ends, so shall there be a Timekeeper. But we cannot live forever. We must choose someone new to take our place. I have chosen you. You see, I foresaw it. And those that came before me saw the prophecy."

"The prophecy?" Lucinda asked.

The Timekeeper stood and led Lucinda over to a cave wall with the most markings of any of them. The woman touched the walls and began to move her fingers over each of the markings.

"We must work to make sure that the prophecy is not fulfilled," the woman said. "It will be the end of everything as we know it. It is a dark prophecy. It states that one of our Timekeepers will be the bearer of this prophecy, bringing it to fruition. Therefore, when you choose your successor, you must be absolutely certain there is no darkness in them."

The woman turned to look at Lucinda, reached up, and touched her cheek.

"They call you Lucinda in the village," she said. "You are a child of the light. I trust you will make the best decisions. Will you accept this responsibility?"

"Why me?" Lucinda asked.

"Because you see the beauty in the world," the Timekeeper said. "I see you stand at those cliffs every day. You are meant to be the next Timekeeper."

"What exactly does this prophecy state?"

"It is a very detailed prophecy," the woman said, "but it starts with the Timekeeper turning against their duty and defiling the powers entrusted to them."

"Defiling?" Lucinda asked.

"Instead of taking sole responsibility," the Timekeeper said, "this Timekeeper is destined to start a society of Timekeepers that will bring about the end, slowly but surely."

"But why?"

4

"That I am not sure of," the Timekeeper said. "There is personal motivation involved I believe. Regardless, the end of the prophecy states that the Timekeeper will reproduce, creating Timekeeper children, and that in this line of descendants, twin girls will be born and brought into the darkness. And they'll rule the world."

No one should have that much power. Lucinda felt it deep in her marrow. It was wrong.

"Do you accept the responsibility then, child?"

Lucinda looked back at the old woman. "Am I allowed to reproduce then?"

The old woman nodded. "Yes. The powers that will be bestowed on you are external only. It also part of the prophecy that the Timekeeper will take on internal powers, and only when these powers are internal can they be passed on to a child born of them."

Lucinda nodded. "I accept then."

The old woman nodded. "Very well. We shall begin your training. I only have a few more years left in me and then this will all be yours. Come."

And so Lucinda started her training. Each day, she would wander off to the Timekeeper's cave. The woman had given her an object of her own that contained the external powers needed to get into the cave—a circular stone necklace that she wore around her neck.

The years began to pass by and the old woman came closer to her death. One day, Lucinda and she were studying in the cave when Lucinda had a premonition about an invasion of the land that her people had settled. She saw the deaths of many of her people.

"I must go to them."

The old woman grabbed her by the wrist.

"You must not stop death," the woman said. "It will upset the balance and cause the world to reset. An Ice Age."

"I can't let my people die," Lucinda said. "And we could find a way to survive that."

Lucinda shook her head. "If you do this, death will still find a way to take the ones you love in addition to upsetting the balance of nature and causing an Ice Age."

"I can't let them die."

Lucinda broke free from the woman's grip and ran to the village. Because her powers were external, she was able to show them the premonition of what was to come. As soon as she had, she could feel the upset of Time, but her people didn't. Instead they began shouting at her.

"Sorcery!" they cried.

And then they took her and her family and tied them up. Before anything else could be done, the invasion began and her family was killed anyway. She was able to escape back to the caves before anything happened to her.

"They thought I was something evil," Lucinda said to the old woman, tears falling down her face.

"Humans fear that which they don't understand," the old woman said. "You must not do that again. We now have to live through the Ice Age."

"Can't we reverse it?" Lucinda asked.

"Yes," the old woman said, "but it requires more than we can spare. It will be fine. We can live through it. But you mustn't do that again.

Do you understand?"

Lucinda nodded. And time passed once more.

Eventually, Lucinda came out of the caves once more during the Ice Age and met a man. The two of them had a child together, and it was at that point Lucinda decided the man needed to be showed the truth.

"I don't know how he will take all of this," Lucinda said to the Timekeeper, now bedridden and close to death.

"I'm sure it will be fine," she said. "If you trust him, then do it."

She did and she brought him and their child to the caves. But the reaction from the man was not the one she had expected. He didn't understand the powers she had been practicing and accused her of tainting their child.

"I promise you," she begged of him, "this power is important for the sake of humanity."

"No!" he shouted. "This isn't right. It isn't natural. I must put our child out of its misery."

She chased him out of the caves and up the cliffs. He had taken her child and was carrying it with him.

"What are you doing?" Lucinda shouted. "Please, don't."

But it was too late. He held the child in his arms and jumped into the sea. The two of them were swept away.

"No!" Lucinda shouted, falling to her knees in agony. Why was this happening? Why couldn't people understand? But she knew the answer to that. They couldn't understand because she was forced to stay in the darkness. Her name meant light. Surely that meant she needed to bring these powers into the light?

Lucinda returned to the cave and looked over the prophecy markings on the wall. And then she went to the old Timekeeper's bed.

"Come with me," Lucinda said, helping the old woman to her feet. She led the woman to the body of water.

"What are we doing?" the woman asked.

"The world won't understand," Lucinda answered. "Unless I show them."

The woman turned to her, realizing what was happening.

"No," she said.

"You are close to death," Lucinda said, "and it says I need to sacrifice a Timekeeper to gain these internal powers. It's okay, this isn't a dark prophecy. It's meant to bring the truth into the light."

"No," the woman said. "You are letting the death of your child blind your judgment. These powers, when they possess you, you will feel no love. You will feel nothing for anyone. You can't do this."

"I have to show people the truth," Lucinda said. "I'm sorry."

And she took out a dagger she had hidden in her robes and stabbed the old woman. The woman let out a groan and fell to the ground, dying. Lucinda dragged her into the water. And then she used the dagger to slice open her hand and let her own blood be mixed with Time. She felt the worst pain she had ever felt and screamed and screamed and screamed. It was as if her body was on fire. Burning, burning, burning. And then, nothing. Her pain, her sadness. It was gone. All of it was gone.

And now it was time for her to watch the world burn.

Part One

Lies
November 1944

CHAPTER ONE

I am not the girl I used to be. I'm not sure if I will ever be that girl again.

Thomas, Alma, Oliver, and I arrived at an airport in Colorado Springs, and we were now in a car taking us up into the mountains. We were about an hour out from Cripple Creek where Thomas' father owned a home on the edge of the little town. Oliver and Alma were in the front seat, Oliver driving, and Thomas sat next to me. I didn't look at him though. My attention was drawn to the window. I watched as the scenery passed me by. It was the early light of morning; the plane ride had taken a good portion of the night and we had rested for it a bit in Colorado Springs before heading out. A year ago, I would have been thrilled, overjoyed even, to be in Colorado, to be seeing the mountains. But now it all felt meaningless.

My grandmother, Lucinda, had accomplished yet another step in her plan. And while I had escaped, I knew that she would stop at nothing until she found me. I wasn't sure if the scarier part was that she was out there looking for me, or that it would foil her plans if I were actually dead. If I died, there would be nothing for her to accomplish. She needed me alive in order for her prophecy to come true. But at the same time, as Thomas had told me over and over again while on the plane, death would be meaningless. Sure, it would foil her plan, but the plan was already in place. What I needed to do now was to figure out how to turn this around. I needed to figure out how I could reverse time, to save all of the innocent people who had perished in San Francisco, as well as the innocent people yet to be lost.

I knew there was a way. I was an original Timekeeper. And according to the rumors, only the original Timekeeping family had the ability to reverse time, to fix the mistakes. The only problem was that I had no idea where our Headquarters had been located. If only Elijah hadn't been—but I stopped myself from thinking it. It was no use. He couldn't help me anymore. I had to figure this out. I knew that my biological mother, Elisabeth Callaghan, was most likely alive. She was out there somewhere. Her brother and sister were both dead now, but she was out there. She had to be. And she would know how to fix this.

I yawned. My eyelids were growing heavy. Even when we had stopped to rest, I hadn't slept. Now felt like the perfect opportunity. Before my eyes shut completely, I noticed a gray-brown bird, with a hint of orange, flying alongside the car. There was something familiar about it—something I knew I should have remembered but couldn't —and it was still on my mind as I nodded off to sleep.

* * *

"We're here."

As soon as Oliver spoke the words, my eyes popped open and I noticed that we were indeed there. I felt groggy from the nap.

I looked out the window and saw that we were pulling up a hill and just ahead was the home of Thomas' father. It was a two-story home, neatly perched at the top of the hill and overlooking the small town.

Oliver honked on the horn as he pulled the car to a stop. The door of the home opened and a man that was almost the exact image of Thomas, but older, stepped through the frame. He waved at us and then came down to the car.

Thomas reached across me and opened the car door, pushing it open.

"After you," he said.

I climbed out of the car and immediately wrapped my arms around myself. It was a bit chillier here, considering the altitude was higher.

"Thomas," Thomas' father said, walking over to his son and wrapping his arms around him.

The father and son held each other for a moment before breaking apart.

"I received your message that you were coming," his father said, "and it seemed urgent."

"It is," Thomas replied. "I apologize that I couldn't be more specific, but there wasn't much time to explain. Dad, you know Oliver, of course, and this is Alma, my latest trainee." Thomas gestured toward Alma and his father held out his hand and shook hers. Thomas then gestured to me. "And this is Abigail. She was also

15

a recent trainee, but she had already been initiated. She's the one I've been writing to you about."

She's the one I've been writing to you about.

I guess I shouldn't have been surprised that he was writing about me. I had, after all, mentioned his name in a few letters to Mathias.

Mathias. My heart almost stopped at the thought of him. He would have surely heard about what happened in San Francisco and have no way of knowing that I got out safely. Why hadn't I thought to send a message to him before we left our pocket watches behind? The thought hadn't even occurred to me because of everything that was going on.

"Abigail?"

I snapped out of my thoughts and looked over to Thomas.

"This is my father," he said, giving me an odd look.

"My apologies," I said smiling.

Thomas' father held out his hand to me. "Henry Jane."

I shook it. His grip was strong, and I could tell he was a confident man, but also likable. He had manners and was friendly.

"It's nice to meet you, sir," I said politely.

"Well enough of this," Henry said. "It's already dropped ten degrees since last night. Something's going on and I heard about what happened in San Francisco on the radio. Come inside and you can explain."

The four of us followed Henry into his home. As soon as I stepped in, I could feel it was an older home. All of Henry's items seemed to have an antique feel to them—as if they had been there for a long time. Pictures adorned the walls of the Jane family. There were pictures of Thomas, a young child with his father and his mother, not his biological mother, as he had previously explained to me, but the woman that had raised him. There were also older pictures of the Jane family. One picture in particular that stood out was of a man dressed in a Civil War uniform. I could only assume that this was Reginald Jane, Thomas' grandfather. As soon as I was reminded of that, my mind flashed back to the sword that Thomas kept in his study at the San Francisco Headquarters. It had been the sword that his grandfather had used in the war. The sword that Council Headrick had pushed into my uncle, killing him. I quickly looked away from the picture and turned my attention back to Henry, who was gathering everyone in his living room.

Henry gestured for all of us to take a seat on the couch, and we did. As soon as I sunk into the cushions, I didn't want to get up again. It was comfortable, almost too comfortable, if there was such a thing. I imagined myself falling asleep there for days and not returning to the mess I had made of everything. But that wasn't an option. It couldn't be.

Thomas' father took a seat as well and looked directly at me.

"Tell me what happened," he said.

I looked to Thomas, who simply nodded to go ahead, and so I launched into the story of what had happened in San Francisco, occasionally adding details from my life in London that were necessary in order for everything to come full circle. If there was one thing I could already tell about Henry, it was that he was an attentive listener. Once I was finished, he allowed himself a few moments, and then spoke.

"You made the right decision in not traveling anywhere by Time Line," he began. "I would say it is definitely their intention to track you. You won't have to worry about being tracked here. My pocket watch was passed on to Thomas, which is now gone, and if Abigail and Alma's were left behind, we are safe here for now. However, not having your pocket watch is also going to make things difficult. You will have to travel the normal way, and that is going to slow down what you need to accomplish, which, from what it sounds like, is to find this original Headquarters and reverse what has happened."

I shook my head. "That's just it, I have no idea where it could possibly be."

"Well, much of our older texts are written in Gaelic," Henry replied, "so it would make sense that it would be in Ireland."

It was then that I remembered Mathias had mentioned that as well. It had been in passing, during one of our lessons, but he had said it.

Henry spoke again.

"Your mother's name Callaghan, being an Irish name, means your best bet is Ireland. Where in Ireland, I have no idea. But that is where you need to go, and the sooner the better."

"I don't think I mentioned her last name," I said.

Henry looked caught off guard for a moment, but quickly overcame it.

"I'm positive you did," he said.

I was sure I hadn't, but I didn't worry about it for now. Maybe Thomas had mentioned it at one point. I also needed to find out about Mathias.

"My father, Mathias, is in Paris," I said. "He has no idea I survived, and I didn't think about sending him a message before we left. What can we do? He needs to be with us on this."

"It might be safer for him just to stay there, Abby," Thomas said.

"What if it isn't though?" I asked. "If the Council is looking for us, he might be the first person they try to get information from. He might not be safe with them."

"Maybe we can find some way to get to him," Thomas said, "but for now we have to hope that he is safe and go from there."

"Until then," Henry started in, "all of you are more than welcome to stay here. As I'm sure you've noticed, there are plenty of rooms. I've also got a change of clothes. My wife's clothes would probably be close to you girls' size, and I'm sure Oli and Thomas can find something in my closet."

I looked around at them all. Everyone looked exhausted. I was exhausted. It made sense to step back for the day and take a break. Get some sleep. But first I needed to take a bath.

"Where's the bathroom?" I asked.

Colorado was cold, and I wasn't prepared for it. I had gotten rather used to the nicer weather in San Francisco, especially after living in London all of my life. The hot bath, however, helped remedy the cold some. I knew the water wouldn't stay warm forever, but I wasn't planning to get out until it did go cold. As I laid in the tub, I stared up at the ceiling of the bathroom and pondered the events of the previous week. Everything had happened so quickly, so unexpectedly.

Bridget was dead. My uncle was dead. But my mother was alive. And my grandmother was also alive, and she was out to destroy everything good about the world. I had come so far in finding out about my biological family in the past year, and now, for the first time, I wanted to rewind everything. I didn't want to just rewind the clock on San Francisco. I wanted to rewind the clock on all of it. To that day, that day I had met Ian at the London Library. If I could go back now, I would have told Phillip that he should just skip work for the day, risk getting fired. I'm sure he would've done it if he'd known what was going to happen.

And then I felt guilty. Because there was so much good that had come out of everything. I had met Thomas, and Alma, and Oli, even though I still didn't know much about him yet. And the way I was feeling about Thomas, well, that was something I thought I'd never feel again. And even Bridget, even though she wasn't here with me anymore, we had mended everything. She had finally been honest with me about everything, and I her. But as soon as everything had been fixed, it had all been destroyed. By me.

I let myself slip below the surface of the water and screamed. I screamed for all of my friends and family that had died. For all of the people who had lost their lives in San Francisco because of what I had done, even if I had done it inadvertently. I let myself feel the pain that their family members must be feeling at this very moment. They might even have family members throughout the world that didn't know anything just yet. That made it all the worse.

When I couldn't breathe any longer, I broke the surface, and then I cried. I let myself feel it all, because I wasn't in that darkness anymore, and I needed to get these feelings out of me. Now was the time to fight.

And I was going to fight like hell.

After the water of the bath had finally run cold, I secluded myself in the guest bedroom Henry had provided. The bathroom was attached to the bedroom, and I had yet to receive any clothes, and I didn't want to put the dirty ones from San Francisco back on, so I laid in my bed and pulled up the covers, wearing nothing. It was something I'd never done before, something I was sure my mother would have been appalled at. But she wasn't here. It was just me now.

The door to the room clicked open, and I pulled the covers up closer and looked over to see Thomas. He placed a pile of clothes on the edge of the bed.

"I brought you these."

"Thank you."

"I'll let you get some rest."

He turned to go, but I called to him.

"Will you stay with me? I mean, while we're here, can you just sleep in here? I'm tired of being alone."

A smile appeared on his face, and for the first time, he actually blushed.

"I'm sorry," I said jokingly, "is the handsome Thomas Jane actually flustered right now?"

"Shut up," he said, grinning. "Jesus Christ, the emotions you bring out of me. I'll go get some cloths I'm borrowing from my father, and maybe, you should, um, put some clothes on."

I looked down at myself, covered by the sheet.

"How'd you know?"

He raised an eyebrow at me. "Seriously?"

"Never mind," I responded. "Go get the clothes."

Thomas grinned again, and then opened the door, closing it behind him.

I pushed the covers aside and went through the clothes he had brought. There were several dresses, a few pairs of pants and blouses, and a night gown. Knowing that everyone else was likely to sleep most of the day, I threw the night gown over my head, placed the clothes in an empty wardrobe that stood across from the bed, and began to walk around the room, looking at various pieces of art and pictures Henry had decorated the room with.

The door clicked open, and Thomas' voice came into the room. "Decent?" he asked.

"Yes, thank you," I replied.

He pushed the door open and then closed it again behind him. In his arms were a pile of clothes that he also placed into the wardrobe. He pulled out a pair of undergarments and carried them to the bathroom.

"Alma and Oli have already gone to sleep," he said, looking over his shoulder. "They were exhausted. I'm going to take a quick bath and then get some shut eye too."

I nodded at him, and he went into the bathroom and placed his clothes on a table near the bathtub. The water came on and then he reappeared in the doorway.

"I'll be out soon," he said, smiling again.

I nodded and he turned, pushing the door behind him, but it didn't quite latch. He didn't appear to notice, so I walked over to the door and grabbed the handle to shut it but was suddenly distracted by him.

Thomas had taken off his shirt, and I was captivated. I had never seen him without his shirt on, and hadn't seen a man shirtless since Phillip. Thomas was more broad-shouldered than Phillip had been, and his muscles were a bit more defined. He turned away so that only his back was visible, and then his pants and underwear came off and I was looking at his bare buttocks. It was then that he saw me in the mirror of the bathroom.

"Really?" he asked.

I quickly turned around, and then chastised myself silently for again not latching the door shut.

"If you wanted to see," he said from the bathroom, "I'll you had to do was ask."

"Oh, shut up," I said, grinning. "I was just trying to shut the door and you distracted me. If you'd get it for me, I'd greatly appreciate it."

"My apologies."

The door clicked shut and I took a deep breath, still smiling, and still wanting to see more.

After Thomas had finished his bath, he had put on his long johns and joined me in bed. He had his arm around me, and we were simply staring into each other's eyes, our breathing slow, and everything was perfect.

"How long can we stay here?" I asked, finally breaking the silence between us.

"As long as we need," Thomas replied. "Believe me, my father doesn't mind. I know he enjoys the company."

"That's great," I responded, "but it's not what I mean. I want you to tell me how long you think we can stay here before—" it was hard to put into words the various things that worried me, but I did my best, "—before Lucinda finds me, or before we have to leave because of time resetting the world."

"I don't know," Thomas replied, "and that's the honest answer. I would say we probably don't want to spend any longer than a week here. Tomorrow, we need to map out exactly what we need to do, exactly where we need to go. And then, we should probably spend a bit of time gathering the necessary supplies, and then we move."

My eyes began to water and I buried my head into Thomas' chest. "This is all my fault."

"No," Thomas said, pushing my chin up so that I had to look him in the eyes again. "Abigail, you were manipulated. You know in your heart that you wouldn't have done this intentionally."

"I know," I said, "I just hate the fact that I let myself be put in that situation, and then Bridget ended up dying anyway. It was all pointless."

"But that was their plan," Thomas responded. "That is exactly what they wanted to happen. Listen, you're tired. You need to sleep. We both do. Let's just try to get some rest, and then we'll worry about the future tomorrow. Okay?"

I nodded. He smiled at me, and then I buried myself into his chest again and nodded off.

CHAPTER TWO

The next day, Thomas took me around Cripple Creek. While he had never lived in the old mining town himself, he had visited several times to see his parents.

"Why are you making me climb these hills?" I asked him as I forced my body to go up yet another hill. He was leading me toward a red bricked building that sat perched up ahead, overlooking the city.

"I'm sorry," Thomas replied, "I just wanted to see it. Besides, we're going to officially be on the run soon enough, so you'll need your exercise."

I laughed. "I thought we were already on the run. And what is this 'it' you are wanting to see?"

Thomas gestured towards the red bricked building we were heading for.

"What is it?" I asked him.

"The St. Nicholas Hospital," Thomas said having finally reached the top of the hill and staring at the building.

Breathing heavily, I stopped next to him and leaned over, trying to catch my breath.

"Why did you want to look at a hospital?" I asked.

Thomas didn't look at me; he simply continued to stare at the building. "It's where my mother died."

Guilt from having complained about walking up a hill consumed me. I stepped closer to Thomas and put my arm around him. He pulled me into him and held me close.

"I'm sorry," I said, leaning up on my toes and whispering into his ear.

"She was my true mother," Thomas said. "I've never wanted to know anything about my biological mother. I've never cared to find out anything about her. She didn't want me, so why should I care?"

"It's okay," I said. "I felt the same way, originally. I thought my biological mother threw me away like I was trash, and I didn't want to find out anything about her. It wasn't until I knew the truth that I needed to know."

Thomas broke away from me and walked away. "Well, it's not like there is anything more to my biological mother. She will always be the woman who abandoned me."

I stood there for a moment before finally catching up to him again. "I wasn't saying that you should feel like you have to go find out about her or anything."

"Well you sure made it sound like maybe my assumptions about her are incorrect," he said. "She abandoned me. She left my father alone. There's nothing more I need to know about her."

I turned away from him and gazed back up at the hospital. For the first time he seemed genuinely angry with me, and I didn't know what to say. I knew there was only one thing to say, and to leave it at that.

"I'm sorry," I said. And then I turned to head back down the hill.

As I walked away, I heard Thomas give a frustrated sigh and then he was by my side and taking my hand.

"Excuse my language," he said, "but it's so fucking impossible to stay angry at you."

He pulled me into him and I smiled as he did.

We had lunch at a small café not too far from the hospital. Really, when I thought about it, everything wasn't too far from everything else because it was such a small town. Being in Cripple Creek felt like being in an entirely different world compared to London and San Francisco.

"This town is so quaint," I said to Thomas as a waitress placed our drinks on the table. "Everyone seems so nice here."

The waitress laughed at my comment. "What's left of them, that is."

I gave her an odd look. "What do you mean?"

"Cripple Creek was a gold mining town," she replied. "At the turn of the century we had over 10,000 people in this town. Now we have a little under 3,000. Mark my words, we'll be a ghost town before long. Gold has gone and dried up."

The waitress laughed again, but there was a hint of sadness to it, and then walked away.

"That's awful," I said to Thomas, looking out the window of the café. "The town is dying. I guess it doesn't matter though, considering what I did to the entire world."

Thomas took my hand in his. "Stop that. We are going to fix this. You know we are. We are going to go to Ireland and turn back time, just like Elijah said."

I shook my head in frustration. "Thomas, even if we did get to Ireland, we have no idea where to look for the original Headquarters. And I have no idea how to get in. I have no idea how to turn back time. We need to find my mother."

He squeezed my hand. "And we will. We will find her. We will find her, and we will fix this."

My eyes began to water. I pulled my hand from Thomas' and quickly rubbed away the tears that were about to fall.

"It's dangerous," I said. "Thomas, I've lost so much already. I can't lose you. I won't lose you."

"What are you saying?" Thomas asked.

I looked him point blank in the eyes. "I'm saying maybe I should go through with this on my own."

He shook his head. "There is no way in hell I'm letting you go through this by yourself. You need me, Abby. You need all of us: Alma, Oli, my father, Mathias, and your mother, Elisabeth."

The tears returned and began to fall down my cheeks. Thomas reached out and brushed them away with his thumb.

"Life used to be so simple," I said, looking out of the window again. "I'm not the girl I used to be."

"Honestly," Thomas replied, "I don't think any of us are going to be the people we used to be. This has changed us all."

I didn't respond. Thomas turned and also looked out the window. I reached out and touched the windowpane.

"It's getting colder," I said.

"It is Colorado."

I shook my head. "No, the temperature just keeps going down. Ask your father and anyone here, I bet it doesn't just drop this fast."

The return of the waitress and placement of our meals on the table brought me out of my thoughts.

"We've been in the negatives before," the waitress said, responding to my comments on the weather, "but that's always at night. Right now, we're already in the single digits. It'll be a record for sure if we get into the negatives today before nightfall. Can I get you anything else?"

Both of us shook our heads in unison and as the waitress walked away, I looked down at my food and played with it with my fork.

"I'm not so hungry anymore," I said.

"Eat up," Thomas said. "Anything could happen, and you'll want to make sure you're nourished and rested." He nodded at my food again. "Eat."

I sighed but gave in and began to eat my food.

The music that had been playing over the radio was suddenly interrupted.

"This just in," the announcer said, "sources are reporting that a devastating earthquake has shaken the entire city of Los Angeles, resulting in a catastrophic loss of human life as well as severe structural damage to some of the city's most iconic buildings. This news comes only a day after the city of San Francisco also suffered severe earthquakes as well as a tsunami. Sources close to us say that there are almost no survivors in the city limits, and that emergency crews are still unable to get into the city because of severe flooding and the potential threat for a second tsunami. We will keep you updated as more comes in about both of these incidents."

I dropped the fork and sat back, looking at Thomas.

"There's no way I can eat now," I said.

He sighed, closing his eyes as if he were thinking, and then opened them again.

"From what Elijah said, we should expect this to continue happening. You can't let it beat you down. We will fix this."

Even though he was right in front of me, he felt a million miles away. I nodded absentmindedly and he continued eating. I turned my attention to the world outside, where the temperature continued to drop. Again, I noticed the gray-brown bird. The kind of bird it was kept slipping my mind. But it brought me a sort of comfort, and I wished I knew why.

CHAPTER THREE

That night, I found myself wide awake at two in the morning. Thomas, on the other hand, was still sound asleep. I carefully maneuvered myself out of his arms, careful not to rouse him.

Once I climbed out of bed, I walked over to the window that overlooked the driveway below where the car we had driven here was parked. Everything looked fairly normal outside, except for the temperature continuing to decline. The house was draftier than it had been when we went to sleep, and I found that my hand was freezing as soon as I placed it on the pane of the window.

Turning toward the bedroom door, I saw a faint light glowing from underneath the threshold. It looked like someone might be up, and being unable to go back to sleep, I decided to investigate.

After stepping out onto the landing and making my way down the staircase, I turned right into Henry's sitting room and found Oliver on the couch. The source of the light was a fire going in the fireplace, and upon closer inspection, I saw that Oliver had what looked like a photo album laid out on his lap. As I crept closer, the floor creaked and Oliver quickly looked over his shoulder.

"You startled me," Oliver said. "Surely I didn't wake you?"

I shook my head. "No, I'm just wide awake and couldn't sleep. I saw a light and came down to check it out. Looks like it was the fire."

"I haven't been able to sleep either," Oliver said. "I'm just looking at some old pictures."

I moved around the edge of the couch and took a seat next to Oliver. The photo album looked old, and the pictures looked even older.

"How long have you known Thomas?" I asked.

"Oh, my entire life. You see, Henry was a pilot in World War I with my father. Our fathers were also pretty close friends. They have several pictures in here together. This is just before Henry met Thomas' birth mother."

"She left Thomas and Henry, didn't she?" I asked even though Thomas had already told me this to be true.

Oliver nodded. He began to page through the album until he found what he was looking for. He pulled out a tattered old photo and handed it to me.

"This was shortly after Thomas was born," he said. "His mother didn't stay long. In fact, I think this is the only picture of her. I know nothing about her. Henry never speaks of her, and never told Thomas her name or anything. I don't think he wants to know."

I reached out and took the picture from Oliver, turning my attention to a younger version of Henry. He was clearly happy, holding his baby in his arms. And then my heart almost stopped as I looked at the woman next to them. She looked as if she wanted nothing to do with the man and child standing next to her. She had short brown hair and wore a plain outfit. She looked exactly the same, albeit younger, as she did when I had let her plunge into the watery depths of the Thames all those months ago.

Thomas' mother was Bessie.

My hand shook as I continued to hold the picture and look into Bessie's eyes.

"Abigail?"

I broke out of my trance and looked back at Oliver. "I'm sorry. Yes?"

"Are you okay?" Oliver asked. "You're shaking."

I handed the picture back to him and stood up. "I'm fine. I just, I just need to get back to bed."

Oliver gave me a puzzling expression but didn't question me. He bid me good night and I made my way back upstairs and into the bedroom I was sharing with Thomas. He was still sound asleep as I entered the room and shut the door. I got back into bed but didn't go to sleep. Instead, I watched Thomas sleep.

Surprisingly, it didn't bother me that Bessie was his mother. You couldn't judge someone because of who their parents were. I thought of Lucinda, my grandmother. And I thought of my sister, Melanie. We all had people in our families that weren't good people. What mattered was the amount of good there was in a family, and the choices those good people made. Those good choices would override the bad.

No, what really bothered me was that Thomas supposedly didn't know that Bessie was his mother. Henry had never mentioned her name, and Thomas would have no idea that the woman in the one picture he had would be Bessie, because he wouldn't know what Bessie looked like. As I watched Thomas sleep, I wondered how this knowledge might change him. I didn't want to do that to him. I didn't want to change him. But I also remembered to how I felt before I knew the truth about my biological parents. I would have wanted to know. Even after everything that had happened to me, I would still want to have known everything I could about them.

Thomas looked so peaceful. I decided that for now, I would keep this knowledge to myself. I reached out to move some hair that had fallen in front of his closed eyes. And then there were flashes.

I saw her. Bessie.

"I'm with child," Bessie was telling a younger version of Henry. They were in the American Headquarters.

"That's great, love," Henry said, kneeling in front of her and taking her hands in his.

Bessie didn't look particularly pleased by the idea.

And then more flashes. She was fully pregnant now, and she was in a bathroom, taking something. And then Henry found her unconscious. And then she was giving birth, and then they were taking the picture that Oliver had just shown me. And then Bessie was trying to smother Thomas in his crib with a pillow.

"What are you doing?" Henry shouted at her.

He pushed Bessie out of the way, and she grabbed something and

34

lunged at him. Thomas was crying during all of this. And then I pulled my hand away and everything stopped. The visions, they melted away as if they hadn't been there at all.

In the darkness, I looked at my hand. I had simply reached to move some hair out of Thomas' eyes, and I had seen into his past. How could this be possible? It was something unlike anything I had experienced thus far as a Timekeeper.

It's another power. Something only original Timekeepers possess.

Melanie.

Leave me alone, I said to her in my mind. I don't want anything to do with you.

You're never going to be safe. We have a connection Abigail.

You haven't spoken to me since San Francisco.

That is your doing. You've kept me at bay. But I can break through when you are most vulnerable. And now I know where you are.

What do you mean?

But she was gone.

I shouted to the room. "What do you mean?"

Thomas jolted upright, looking around in the darkness, and then turning on the bedside lamp.

"Abby?" he asked, reaching for me.

"Thomas," I said, turning to him, "I think she knows. I think Melanie knows where we are. We have to go."

Thomas looked at me for a brief second, a questioning look on his face, and then he jumped out of bed and sprang into action.

"I should have considered this," Thomas said, throwing on his shirt and pants. "Part of your connection is the ability to know what you're thinking. She can see your thoughts when you let her in, and I'm sure you had some brief thought of Colorado in there, even if you didn't mean to."

"But I can't see her thoughts," I countered, completely dumbfounded by what was going on.

Thomas stopped what he was doing and walked over to me. He sat next to me.

"Abby," he said, touching my shoulder, "she's had years and years of training. They've been preparing her for this. She's going to know exactly how to get into your head, especially when you are vulnerable, and she's going to know exactly how to keep you out of hers. Did something happen while I was asleep? Something had to have broken you down."

I quickly shook my head. "Nothing."

I hated lying to him.

He considered me for a moment and then stood up again, moving about the room and grabbing things he thought we might need.

"Surely we have some time though," I said. "They have to travel by Time Line to get here right? There's no Time Line in Colorado, I'm assuming."

"No," Thomas said, finding a suitcase in a closet. "But remember, the Time Line can drop you anywhere you want to go. They could be here in a matter of minutes, especially if they've got Headrick on their side. I've no doubt she's probably gotten out of Antarctica and back to her place at the Central Headquarters. From there, she has access to tools that will allow her to travel anywhere. They will be here within a matter of minutes."

At that, I sprang into action. "I'll wake everyone."

"Wake up my father, too," Thomas said. "He'll need to go with us or they will charge him with conspiring against the Council, I've no doubt about it."

I left the room and moved quickly down the hallway, opening doors and turning lights on. Alma walked out of her room, and Henry walked out of the other. Oliver appeared at the foot of the stairs.

"Was goin' on?" Alma said, rubbing her eyes from being pulled from a deep sleep.

"We need to leave," I told them all. "They know where we are. My sister, Melanie, read my mind. They're coming."

Alma, Henry, and Oliver looked at me for a second, and then they all sprang into action, moving from room to room to get their things together.

Thomas appeared in the doorway of our room.

"Abby," he said, "I need you to tell me where to go. Finding your mother is our best bet at figuring all of this out. Where do you think she is?"

I shook my head. "I don't know. I honestly have no idea where she could be."

Thomas stepped forward and put his hands on my shoulders. "We need to have a place to go. We can't just run from one place to another."

"Don't you think I know that? Thomas, if I knew where she might be, I'd tell you. I'm not going to just make a random guess though and send us all on a wild goose chase."

"Paris."

Thomas and I turned to look at Henry. He was standing at the far end of the hallway, a suitcase already in his hand. He looked as if he had just let out a secret that he had been keeping for the longest time.

I looked at him, confused. "What did you say?"

"Your mother," he responded, "she's in Paris. I'm absolutely positive about that. We don't have the time for me to give the whole story, but I know your mother, and I promised to keep her location a secret unless it was urgent it be revealed. I wasn't sure at first whether or not I should say anything, but I know now that it's best to reveal where she is. And since Mathias is there as well, maybe we can find a way to get to them both."

Thomas was completely still next to me. He was also confused by this revelation, but he didn't question it.

"Very well," he said. "We will go to Paris. Let's hurry."

Thomas went back into the room and Henry proceeded down toward me, brushed past me, and headed down the stairs. I turned and stood at the foot of the stairs, looking down at him.

"Mr. Jane," I called after him, "how do you know my mother?"

He turned and looked back at me, a look of sadness on his face. "Please, now isn't the time Abigail, but I promise you, you can trust me. And please, call me Henry." He walked on, disappearing from my sight, leaving me at the top of the stairs, briefly wondering who he really was.

As soon as we possibly could, we were all packed together into the car and heading back for Colorado Springs. Oliver knew someone who could get us a larger plane, and he would fly us to Paris. Since Mathias also was in Paris, we would find a way to get to him as well. How, I had no idea. And it almost seemed like it would be harder getting to him for once than to my mother who had faked her own death.

Henry drove the car, with Oliver in the front passenger seat. Alma, Thomas, and I were in the back. I looked out the window as the car moved on toward our destination. It had begun to snow, quite heavily.

"This isn't good," Oliver said, looking out the window. "They aren't going to let us take off if visibility is this reduced."

"I don't think we have much of a choice, Oli," Thomas replied from the back seat. "There might not even be anyone there to stop us. If it keeps up, they might have shut down the airport by the time we get there."

I was seated between Alma and Thomas. Alma turned to me and smiled.

"How are you doing?" she asked me. "We haven't had much chance to talk since we got here."

I returned the smile. "I'm fine. I just hate that all of you have to go through this with me."

Alma clasped my hand in hers. "I want to go through this with you. If we can turn things around, and get these dark Timekeepers out of the Council, I think things could get a lot better for everyone. Even though the Timekeepers are more accepting of my people than the everyday human being, it still isn't great."

I nodded at that, remembering quite clearly Stuart Winston's blatant discrimination.

"Alma," I said, "can I ask you something?"

She nodded.

"Have you ever touched something and then had some sort of memory about it?" I asked her.

"I haven't," Alma said. "But I've heard about the ability. I think it's called being an empath or something like that. I haven't heard of Timekeepers possessing the ability though, but more so in science fiction. Did you experience something like that?"

I wanted to say yes. I wanted to tell her that I had experienced something. But I didn't. Instead I just shook my head.

"No," I said, "I just saw something about it in a book and was curious. Forget I asked."

Alma gave me a questioning look but didn't say anything more about it. She turned to look out the window, and after a bit, fell asleep.

I relaxed my head on Thomas' shoulder. He too had been staring out the window. He placed his arm around my neck and I scooted closer to him. I wanted to throw my arms around him, but I didn't. He was right there with me, but I was afraid that I was going to lose him. I couldn't lose him. I couldn't lose him or anyone else. I fell asleep against him, with the fear of my loved ones on my mind.

Henry and I sat in an area of the Colorado Springs Airport. It wasn't a passenger waiting area, as the airport had been taken over by the military for purposes relating to the war. Thomas and Oliver had gone to speak with someone in the military that they had a connection with, to hopefully find a plane that Oliver could operate and use to fly us to Paris. Alma had gone off to look around for a bit, and I found myself sitting alone for the first time with Henry. He didn't speak at all. The only sounds he made were the sounds of breathing and the nervous tap of his foot against the concrete floor.

After sitting there for about ten minutes, I finally turned to him.

"How do I know I can trust you?" I asked him.

The foot tapping stopped, and he didn't look at me right away. He gazed off into the distance, looking at nothing in particular. I assumed he was pondering his answer. Finally, after what looked like an internal struggle, he reached into the inside pocket of his jacket and pulled out a bundle of envelopes.

My breathing became ragged. The envelopes were all of various colors, postmarked from various places, but they all had the same familiar handwriting. Handwriting I had already seen on the letter my mother left for my adoptive parents, the letter telling me my father was dead, because she wanted to keep me away from the world of the Timekeepers.

"Are those from her?"

It took everything in my power not to snatch them out of Henry's hand. They weren't mine after all, whatever claim I felt I had on them.

Henry looked at them, and then back at me, and nodded. He looked like he was struggling to hand them to me, like he was struggling to give up part of his soul. Finally, he did.

"I wish I could give you an explanation," Henry said. "I wish I could tell you everything. It's not that I can't. I just don't feel that I'm strong enough. And I'm sure you'd rather hear it from her."

Henry stood up and walked away, not looking back at me. I had only known him for a day, but so far he was surprising me in so many different ways. I turned my attention back to the envelopes and began to sift through them, until I found the earliest one I could. I opened it, took a deep breath, and began reading.

January 30, 1926

My Dearest Henry,

I miss Mathias. I miss my daughters. I miss London. I miss you.

Even though I am left with the pain and guilt of my decisions, I still know I made the right ones. I take comfort in knowing Abigail is safe from my mother, and that Mathias, while I'm sure is suffering, is also safe. I grieve every day that I wasn't able to save my other daughter. I'm not sure if I'm a believer in anything, but I want to be one. I pray every single day that my other daughter will be safe, that she will somehow get away from my mother, Bessie, and Aldridge. But I've also been on this earth long enough to know not everything you hope for will come true.

It has taken everything in my power not to go searching for them myself. For I know if I do this the plans I put in place for Abigail's safety will be for nothing. It also pains me to think of the other adoptive family that you had in mind, and how they will never get to see their child, nor know what happened to her.

My dear Eleanor. She sacrificed so much for me. So, so much. And for what in return? The most heinous of deaths? And the worst part of it all is that I know if she were here, she'd do it again. The things we do for the ones we love.

I hope you're doing well, and I hope that your son is doing well also. I know you were worried about how he would turn out. I'm confident in my marrow he'll be fine. You're giving him such a good life. He will be fine. And you will be fine.

Though we never acted on our feelings for each other, I want you to know I've always loved you. And while it may seem like I chose, I never did.

Thank you for keeping my secret.

Love,

E.

When I looked up from the letter, I realized that my eyes were burning. I had been crying. I looked back at the letter and reread different parts. The part that caught my attention the most, was where she acknowledged that she had been in love with Henry. She stated they had never acted on their feelings, which I took to mean she had always been faithful to my father. But she had loved more than just him. And there was a certain comfort in that—in knowing it was okay to love more than one person, that you couldn't help it. And while my situation was different, it made me feel better about loving Thomas, even though I was still in love with Phillip, and even though I might always be in love with Phillip. That was what life was.

I closed my eyes, took a deep breath, and then tucked the letters into the bag I was carrying with me. I would read them. Not all at once, but I would read them. And I would meet her. I was going to meet my mother. Nothing would stop me.

CHAPTER FOUR

"We got a C-47 Skytrain."

I looked up as Oliver appeared, followed by Thomas and Henry.

I raised an eyebrow at him. "I'm sorry?"

Thomas smiled. "We've got an airplane."

And then I felt it. Hatred. Pure hatred. Evil. I closed my eyes and leaned forward. It was almost as if I was getting sick and throwing up the contents of my stomach. My hands went up to my ears to try and muffle the screaming I was hearing, but I knew that would be no use. The screaming was coming from within me. Not outside of me.

"Abigail?"

I felt Thomas' hands on my shoulders.

"Are you okay?" he asked, massaging my shoulders gently.

I shook my head. "She's here. Melanie's here. I can feel her."

Thomas abruptly stood up and announced to the room, "We need to go. Where's Alma?"

"She went to the restroom," Oliver said. "I'll find her. The rest of you get outside to the runway."

"Come on," Thomas said, pulling me up.

As soon as I stood, however, I crippled over onto the floor. I had no idea what she was doing to me, but it was unbearable. Feeling evil and hatred, it felt like knives stabbing you all over your body. Over and over and over again they stabbed you. But you never died. It felt like never ending torture.

"I don't think I can walk," I muttered. "I don't know what she's doing to me."

And then suddenly Thomas was carrying me, and we were running to the stairs that would take us down to the runway where the plane was waiting. I put my hands around Thomas' neck to steady myself.

As soon as we were outside, snow was slamming into our faces. It was a literal blizzard. And it was freezing. I shivered in Thomas' arms. I looked ahead and saw the plane in front of us. It was a bronze color, with W7 written on the side of it. A door on the side of the plane, toward the back, was open and waiting for us to enter through it.

A man's screams erupted out of nowhere. These weren't in my head. Thomas turned around and there was Henry buckling over on the ground behind us. He was drastically aging. It was one of the Forbidden Powers. Not far behind him was Lucinda. Her blonde hair blew in the wind of the blizzard. She wore a long, blue coat tied around her waist. As always, she wore heels that could be heard clicking against the concrete, even in the sounds of the blizzard. And the blizzard wasn't keeping her back. She continued to move forward, her piercing, blue eyes concentrated on Henry.

Thomas turned and headed for the plane. "Shit, shit, shit." He was running now. As soon as he reached the entrance to the plane, he placed me safely inside and then ran back for Henry. The pain that I had been feeling from Melanie slightly subsided. I assumed we had put a little distance between us, wherever it was they were keeping her. When I turned back to look out of the plane, I still only saw Lucinda, using her powers on Henry. She took one look at Thomas running to save his father, and he too went down.

"Thomas!" I shouted.

Lucinda's attention turned toward me, and she began walking through the blizzard once more, past the two men she had sent buckling in pain to the ground. She was determined as she marched. She looked like an unstoppable queen of ice, her blonde hair whipping around her face, her piercing gaze on me. I'd had about enough of this. I forced myself up and exited the plane and made a run toward Lucinda. She didn't stop marching toward me and I could feel her trying to use her power on me. But it wasn't as strong. Because it wasn't meant to be used on me. I was an original Timekeeper. Just keep moving, I told myself. Keep moving. I ran and ran toward her and then I pushed my body right into her, taking us both toward the ground.

My thought process was correct. She hadn't expected I'd do that and her concentration was lost. Thomas and Henry were standing up now.

"Hello, grandmother," I said, looking down at her.

"You stupid girl," Lucinda said to me.

"Am I the stupid one?" I asked her. "You clearly didn't bring enough provisions to help you take me back today."

She laughed at me. "I think you'll be surprised. Haven't you noticed that your little friends aren't here with you?"

But then they were. I looked up and they were running toward us. I smiled and looked back at Lucinda. She was clearly displeased.

"What are you going to do then?" she asked me. "Are you going to kill me?"

Closing my eyes, I put my hands around Lucinda's neck. I couldn't look at her as I did it. This wasn't me, but I couldn't allow her to keep killing people, to fulfill whatever she wanted me to fulfill.

She began to slacken beneath my grip, but then she managed four words that made me stop.

"You need me alive."

My eyes widened. "What do you mean?"

She laughed at that, and then everyone appeared at my side.

"I need a weapon," I said, looking up at them all.

They all looked at each other, clearly unsure what to do.

"Does anyone have a weapon?" I demanded, almost screaming.

Finally, Oliver reached into his bag and pulled out a knife.

"Get on the plane," I told them, taking the knife from Oliver.

"I'm not leaving you here," Thomas said to me.

I stared them all down and said firmly, "Get. On. The. Plane. I'm right behind you."

They all looked at each other and then turned, running toward the plane. I looked back at Lucinda, putting the knife against the edge of her throat.

"What do you mean?" I said to her.

She only smiled and so I dug the knife a bit deeper, making a small cut, and making her eyes grow wide.

"I sealed the original Headquarters," she said. "Only I can open it. And you need me alive."

No. No, no, no.

"You're lying," I said, pressing the knife even harder.

Even though her life was in my hands, she grinned a wicked smile at me. "Maybe, but I'd hate for you to kill me and then be stuck in this world. All that death on your hands."

I hit her then. A rage came through me and I hit her. It didn't kill her, but it left her unconscious. I stood up, pocketed the knife, and ran toward the plane. The blizzard was only getting stronger. When I reached the plane, I looked back and saw Lucinda's figure on the concrete and another person coming out of the blizzard. Ian.

He knelt down beside Lucinda and cradled her. As if she meant everything to him. And then he looked at me.

"Go," I said to Oliver as I jumped into the plane. He had positioned himself in the pilot's seat. "Go now!"

Thomas stepped forward and shut the door, closing us off from the world.

"Let's hope to God we don't die in take off," Oliver said, starting up the engine of the plane. "Not like we have a choice."

"One good thing about all of this," Thomas said, "they can't travel back by Time Line now."

A smile lit up my face at that. I remembered what Thomas had told me about traveling with the Time Line. It could drop you in any location that you requested, but if there wasn't a Time Line there, you were stuck getting back the old fashioned way. The only Time Line in America right now, was technically under water in San Francisco.

The plane began to move down the runway, faster and faster and faster. And then we were up in the air. I looked out the windows of the plane. We were going up through the blizzard, and then we were out of it. Above the clouds. In the air. Safe.

At least for now.

"What are you doing?"

Lucinda stood near the cliff's edge, the man she loved perched precariously on it, holding their newborn child.

"Evil!" he shouted at her.

Lucinda shook her head, tears falling from her eyes.

"No," she said, "I'm just like you, except I have this ability."

"Liar!" he shouted. "It's sorcery. It goes against nature and creation! And now you've tainted our child with it. I won't let you defile him."

The man stepped back.

"Please don't," Lucinda said, "please. I promise you I'm good. I would never hurt our child."

The man simply shook his head and then he stepped off the cliff and was gone.

"NO!" Lucinda shouted, running to the cliff's edge as if she could stop them, but she couldn't look. She couldn't. She fell to her knees and screamed a guttural cry from within.

* * *

"Lucinda."

Someone was calling her back. Lucinda's head was pounding, but she forced herself to open her eyes, and she found she was back at the airport, the wind howling and the snow slapping her in the face. She realized Ian was leaning over her and pushed herself up.

"I heard what you told her," Ian said.

Lucinda nodded. "It's how we will all come together in the end."

"But we don't have time," Ian said. "She could wait us out."

Shaking her head, Lucinda looked up at Ian and smiled. "What is the one thing that would her get her to come to us?"

Ian looked back at where the plane had taken off and then back at Lucinda.

"Thomas," he said, "but how?"

"That boy is Bessie Watson's child," Lucinda said. "Bessie told me this long ago, but I didn't believe her until now. I saw her in him."

"They don't look that much alike," Ian said.

"Dear," Lucinda said sweetly, but with a hint of poison to it, "when you've been on the earth for over 10,000 years, you can tell things like that. That boy's mother is Bessie, and when he finds out, it will destroy him. He'll be vulnerable. And Abigail, well, she doesn't want to tell him. She's afraid of how he'll react, how it'll change him. Let him be angry, let him confront her, let him leave her. And then, we'll take him. And only then will she come willingly."

"Lucinda," Melanie said, walking up to them. She had been kept hidden, just in case, from everything that had taken place. "They are going to Paris."

"That's where her father is," Headrick said, also appearing at their side, rubbing the back of her head. "They took me by surprise and knocked me out."

Lucinda turned away from them, staring out at the empty openness. "They were stronger than I thought. But not to worry. We'll have them. And Paris, you say?"

"It's not him though," Melanie said. "They aren't going there for him. They are going for someone else."

Lucinda gave her a questioning look. "Who?"

"That's the strange thing," Melanie responded, "I can't see it. Every time I try to, it's like there's a smoke screen."

Surprisingly, Lucinda smiled at this. "Her powers are growing. She's protecting something."

"They think we are stuck here," Melanie said, laughing. "They don't seem to realize the full scope of our power."

Lucinda stood now, brushing the snow off. "Of course, they don't. But they will."

"Excuse me!"

All of them turned to see a police officer heading toward them. "What do you think you all are doing?"

Lucinda reached into the pocket of her coat, clutching a dagger in her hand. She walked up to the officer, holding out her free hand, and freezing him in place. And then she removed her dagger and slide the blade across the man's throat.

"Nothing, officer," she whispered innocently in his ear as his blood spilt to the concrete.

Lucinda held her hand out over the blood and used the energy of Time to create a temporary Time Line.

"To Paris we go," she said, nodding at the others to step into the Time Line.

Once we were up in the air, I sat next to Thomas and Alma on a bench that lined the interior of the plane. It was normally used as a cargo plane, so there wasn't a place to technically sit and be comfortable.

"It's going to get cold in here," Thomas said, pulling some blankets out of the bags he brought with him. He handed one to Alma and one to me.

"What happened?" Alma asked, looking at me. "It didn't look like you killed her."

I shook my head. "I couldn't."

Everyone needed to know this. Henry looked back from the pilot's seat, listening, ready to communicate what I said to Oliver if needed.

"Lucinda told me that she sealed the original Headquarters," I said. "So even if we get there, we can't open it. And the only way to open it is with her. She has to be alive."

"She could be lying," Alma said.

"I know, but I don't think she is. One way or another, this all ends there, with her, and with me. But from here on out, should we encounter her again, as much as it pains me to say this, we have to keep her alive. Or we are all dead."

"What happened with you?" I said, looking to Alma. "You weren't with us."

"Headrick found me," Alma replied. "But Oliver and Henry got her away from me. And we got out."

"Did you see my sister?" I asked her.

Alma shook her head. "No."

I looked away from her. I knew that they wouldn't want Melanie in the action. They were keeping her safe. If anything happened to her, or me for that matter, their whole plan would be destroyed. There would be no more prophecy.

It struck me how ironic it was that they needed Melanie and I alive for their plans and I needed Lucinda alive.

"Everyone get comfortable," Oliver announced from the cockpit. "We're in for a long ride. I'm just hoping we won't hit any rough weather along the way."

If we did hit rough weather, it could be blamed on me. Everything could be blamed on me.

It occurred to me that I was shivering from the freezing temperatures when Thomas put his arm around me and pulled me close to him. He quickly fell asleep, his head resting on my shoulder. I let myself slip into the comfort of his embrace as I contemplated everything I knew about the prophecy, Lucinda, and my mother. My mother. The letter she had left me. I still had it. And in it, she had mentioned her own mother.

I quickly reached for the pocket watch she had left for me. It was safely clasped around my neck, but I had stowed the letter inside it. I was glad I had. My heart hurt as I realized all of my other possessions, things my parents and Phillip had given me, were now under water in San Francisco. Even if I did fix this, how far back would everything be fixed? Was it possible to undo so much damage? So much heartbreak? So much death?

I brushed the thoughts aside and opened the pocket watch, letting the letter tucked inside fall into my lap. I unraveled and reread the words.

Whoever reads this has taken my daughter in. For that I thank you. I only have two requests that I hope you will honor. First, name her Abigail. It was my mother's name. Second, please tell her when she asks about her biological family (if she ever asks) that she has none. After I am finished writing this, she won't. I will be dead within the next few hours. Her father died not long after I was with child. We had no living relatives. Please care for her as if she were your own biological child. Her birthday is December 8, 1925.

-Her mother.

Most of the letter had been falsified. I knew that. She had said that Mathias was dead so I wouldn't meet him, so I wouldn't be initiated, so I wouldn't set the prophecy in motion. But Mathias hadn't known that, and Ian had been working against him. Everything she had done, all the sacrifices she had taken, had been for nothing. But the one thing that baffled me about the letter was that she said I was named after her mother. Her mother's name was Lucinda, not Abigail. I realized she could have easily been lying about this too, but it seemed so trivial a thing to lie about. Why not just say my name was Abigail? Why add a lie about it being her mother's name? There was something to this I was missing.

Sighing, I folded the letter back up and tucked it inside the pocket watch. I lifted my legs onto the bench and laid down. Resting my head in Thomas' lap, I stared up at the ceiling and thought about everything, trying to wrap my mind around it all. But I was exhausted. No matter how much sleep I had gotten over the past few days, I was constantly exhausted. And slowly, I nodded off to sleep.

At some point I woke up. Henry and Oliver were still in the cockpit, flying us to safety. I was no longer in Thomas' lap. Instead he had laid down on his side and pulled me close to him, his arms around me. I carefully slipped out of his arms and stood up, rubbing my hands over my arms. The plane was freezing.

I sat down across from where Thomas was sleeping and watched him. A part of me felt guilty that I hadn't told him about Bessie being his mother. But thinking about it, there really hadn't been any free time to talk about it. Almost as soon as I had found out about it, Melanie had found out where we were and we had to go. I would tell him. I didn't know when, but I would. I reached into my bag and pulled out the next letter that my mother had written to Henry. Every letter of hers brought me closer to her. I carefully removed the letter from the envelope and began to read:

December 8, 1926

Henry,

How are you? I know you won't be able to respond to this letter, but it still comforts me to write this as if you were going to. I hope this letter finds you happy and that you've found some solace in raising Thomas. I know it must hurt not to have a mother figure in his life.

Guess what! I'm in New York City. I left a photo for you. I've never gotten to see the Statue of Liberty before. It was beautiful.

As I write this, my heart pangs as it is the first birthday of my girls. I take comfort in knowing that one of them is doing well, being raised by a couple that loves her. But my heart continues to hurt for the loss of the other. I can't imagine what it is like to be raised by my mother. Of course, I do know. But I at least had my brother and sister, and Abigail. Melanie has no one.

I'm planning to travel across America. I will be in San Francisco at some point. Maybe we'll run into each other? Wouldn't that be lovely?

Hope you are well.

Love,

E.

Abigail. My mind spun. Who was this person I was named after?

I folded the letter back up and placed it back inside the envelope. Also tucked inside the envelope was the picture she had spoken of. My mother was standing in front of the Statue of Liberty on Ellis Island. The smile on her face was bright and cheery, but I could tell she wasn't the same. There was a pain that hadn't been there before. Her hair was pulled up and she was wearing a large hat, I assumed to disguise her identity as much as possible, just in case. I wondered what she would be like when I found her. Would she be happy to see me? Would she be proud of the woman I had become? I wasn't proud. I kept thinking back to everything that had happened in San Francisco. I caused that. And it all could have been avoided. I had gone looking for this world she had tried to keep from me. How could she possibly be proud of that?

I wiped the tear that slipped down my cheek and put the picture back in the envelope and all of the letters back into my bag.

"Are you okay?"

My head swiveled up in surprise at the sound of Alma's voice. I hadn't realized she was awake. She sat across from me, hugging her knees in the cold.

"I'm fine," I responded. I wasn't. What I had found out about Thomas was eating at me, and I had no one to talk to. I certainly couldn't talk to Thomas about it. Not yet at least. If Bridget were here, I could talk to her.

Bridget.

A great sadness came over me when I thought about her. With everything that had happened, I really hadn't taken the time to mourn for her. She didn't even get to have a proper funeral. Did anyone even see her, or check on her, before the entire city flooded? Had she just been left there, completely forgotten? Alma made a slight movement and I realized I had stopped speaking with the intention of saying more.

I looked her in the eye. "Can I ask you something, hypothetically?"

She smiled. "You can ask me anything you'd like."

"If you found something out about the person you loved, something that might crush them, would you tell them?"

"I'd tell them anything," she said.

"But even if this, if this changed everything about them. Everything they had come to know?"

Alma gave me a questioning look. "This is hypothetical?"

I shrugged and she looked over at Thomas and then back at me. "All secrets have a price Abby. Something that you're describing, if I didn't tell the person I loved, I feel it would change them more than if I hadn't. It would change our relationship. The trust we've developed between each other."

I nodded. I knew I would tell Thomas. I would. But just not now. Not like this. With the world the way it was. But I would.

57

CHAPTER FIVE

Turbulence woke me up. At some point during the night, Alma and I had gone back to sleep.

"Is everything alright?" I asked to everyone attempting to sit up.

"We hit a bit of a rough patch," Thomas said. He was still sitting next to me, but it appeared he had woken up hours ago as he was reading a book.

"We're making our descent at the Le Bourget Airport," Oliver said from the cockpit. "I radioed when we were within distance and told them we needed to make an emergency landing. Let's hope they don't ask too many questions."

"Has it been that long already?" I asked, amazed that I'd slept through almost the entire journey.

"You were out cold the entire time," Alma said, still sitting across from me.

"You haven't been getting as much sleep as the rest of us,"

Thomas said. "You needed it."

"Everyone buckle up," Henry said. "We're almost there."

As the plane gradually made its descent, there was more bumpiness, and then we hit the runway. We were in Paris. I'd only been once, as a little girl, with my parents on holiday. I'd loved it and I wished I was returning for a better reason then needing to save the world.

The plane continued moving on the runway for a few moments, and finally we came to a stop. Henry and Oliver left the cockpit, going over to open the doors. Before they did, Henry turned and addressed all of us.

"Oliver and I will take care of the questions," he said. "We were given clearance to land, but I'm sure they will still be suspicious. The rest of you find a place for us and wait inside the airport."

The door opened then, and Oliver and Henry stepped out first and headed to the airport security approaching our plane. The rest of us made our way into the terminal, showed our passports, and then found a place to sit.

"Where do we go next?" Thomas asked as we sat down.

"I suppose Henry will have the answer for that," I said.

He nodded and the three of us waited patiently. Alma was looking out the window and she appeared a bit somber. I reached out and touched her arm.

"Are you alright?"

She turned, smiling, but her eyes were a bit watery. "This is the first time I've ever been anywhere except for America and my home country. It makes me feel somewhat liberated and free to be able to go to different places like this. I've always heard that the City of Lights has been a place of freedom for African Americans, obviously not for the past couple of years though."

"I'm glad that you are able to finally feel welcome in a place," I said. "I hope you know that you're always welcome anywhere with me."

"Thank you," Alma said quietly.

Henry and Oliver entered the terminal at that moment.

"All cleared up," Henry said. "When we were in the air, we told them that we were escaping Colorado and we just updated them about everything since then. Apparently since we've been gone, Colorado Springs has been completely wiped out by one of the worst blizzards they've ever seen. Weather-related tragedies are slowly making their way across the country and the entire system is collapsing. People are robbing stores without any care or thought of breaking the law, their instinct is simply to survive. It's slowly spreading."

"Dad," Thomas said, gesturing toward me.

I had stood up while Henry had shared the news and was looking out at the City of Lights, wondering what terrible tragedy would befall it.

"It's fine," I said. "It keeps me going."

Turning around, I looked toward Henry. "Where can we find my mother?"

"The University of Paris," Henry replied. "She's been a professor of literature there for many years now."

A professor of literature. She loved books as much as I did. She was studying literature just as I had.

That was where we needed to go, but first, we needed to get Mathias.

"We need to find a way to get Mathias first," I said. "Any ideas? Is he living at the Paris Headquarters, or just working there? We never had the opportunity to figure all of that out when it happened."

"How would we possibly get in there though?" Alma asked. "We're basically fugitives in the Timekeeping world."

"I have a contact at the Paris Headquarters," Thomas said. "I know she won't be falling for whatever Headrick is spreading about us. And she lives in the city, not at the Headquarters, so I could pay her a visit and see if she could relay a message."

Henry nodded. "That sounds like an excellent idea. Thomas, do you want to do that with Oliver, and then Alma, Abigail, and I can head to the university and find Elisabeth?"

Thomas nodded and we finalized our plans, making the Eiffel Tower our meetup location.

Before Thomas could go any further though, I took his hand and pulled him back to me.

"Come back to me," I said, and then I leaned up and kissed him.

He smiled against my kiss. "I will. I promise."

And with that, we parted ways.

After arriving at the University of Paris, I left Alma and Henry outside, and entered alone. I used a pair of books I'd brought along with me as a prop and acted like a lost student, hoping Elisabeth would be teaching a class right now. I was in luck. A French girl with jet black hair and glasses asked me if I needed any help. I had learned French growing up and told her I was a student of Professor Durand, the name Henry had told me my mother was using here. The girl quickly led me in the right direction and we found that my mother was indeed teaching a class. The girl left me outside a pair of double doors and I hesitated for a moment, closing my eyes and taking a deep breath, before reaching out and pulling one of the doors open.

The lecture hall was much larger than anything I had been in when I attended Birkbeck. Visually, it was breathtaking. The hall itself was circular, with levels and levels of seats rising up around the center of the room where my mother, Elisabeth Callaghan, stood lecturing her students in her British Literature class. They were discussing, ironically enough, Charles Dickens' *A Tale of Two Cities* and because the class focused on British Literature, everyone was speaking in English, rather than French.

All of those thoughts left my mind however as I looked down at my biological mother for the first time. She was as beautiful as she had always been in my dreams. And she was everything I had imagined her to be—beautiful, educated, and independent.

Discreetly, I made my way to an empty chair at the back of the hall and took my seat.

"Sacrifice," Elisabeth said to her students, "is a common theme in classical literature and it comes up more than once in Dickens' novel. Can anyone tell me how the theme of sacrifice makes its appearance throughout the book?"

Elisabeth placed a copy of the novel that she had been holding as she talked on the table behind her, and leaned against it, folding her arms and waiting patiently.

"Several of the characters sacrifice something important to themselves," a girl at the front of the class said.

Elisabeth nodded. "So they do. Can you elaborate?"

"I mean there is the fact that Sydney Carton sacrifices *himself* in order to save Darnay and his family," the girl said.

A smile lit up Elisabeth's face. She was proud of her students. She looked around the room. "Any other examples?"

There was silence. I was surprised no one was questioning whether or not Carton's sacrifice was a true sacrifice, or whether it was laced with his own self-doubt and self-worth about himself. But nobody said anything. So I decided to.

"Do you really consider Carton's death the ultimate sacrifice though?" I asked the girl.

All eyes turned to me. The girl looked taken aback. "Of course. He could have fallen in love with Lucy after her husband's death."

"Yes, but it was noted over and over again by Dickens that Carton was a drunk. He doubted his abilities. This was constantly emphasized throughout the text, but at the end of it all, we don't know if Lucy reciprocating his feelings would have actually made him a better person. And Carton knew this when he did what he did."

I looked back at Elisabeth and she was staring at me dead on. She knew who I was. I could tell. Her students looked back to her as well and she quickly regained her composure.

"Excellent discussion, everyone," she said. "I think we will call it a day. Please finish up your essays and have them ready by next class.

Good day to you all."

The noise in the room increased as the students started gathering up their materials, closing their books, and putting things into their bags. They began to file out of the room, and within minutes it was cleared. I stood and walked down to the center of the classroom where the lecture area was, my heart beating rapidly in my chest. The woman I had always assumed to be dead was alive. She was alive and in front of me. Elisabeth had her back turned to me, gathering up papers at her desk.

"I know you know who I am," I said.

She stopped, and as she did, I took a moment to reflect on how different she looked compared to the dreams I had of her and the pictures I had seen of her. In my dreams, she had always worn a dress, yet now she wore a blouse and black pants. But the key difference in her appearance was her blonde hair. She had cut most off it and now sported a short, styled look.

"Why are you here?" she asked.

The words weren't the ones I expected. I expected her to throw her arms around me, to embrace me. She hadn't seen me in so many years. But instead she wanted to know why I was here? Finally, she turned around.

As she did, I looked upon her face. It was the same, but older. There were lines in her forehead, from worry no doubt, and she had some wrinkles around her eyes that were slightly concealed by makeup, but still there.

"Because I need your help."

Elisabeth shook her head in frustration. "She found you, didn't she? My mother."

I nodded.

Elisabeth screamed a cry of fury and pushed all the contents of her desk to the floor. Books and papers spilled everywhere. Something breakable had been on the desk as well and shattered as soon as it hit the ground.

"I should have just taken you with me," she said, attempting to choke back tears. She quickly brought her sleeve up to her eyes and wiped away the tears. And then she stepped forward and pulled me into her. My arms came up instinctively around her and I held her close, so close, I didn't want her to go away. Never again. I took in her scent. Peppermint. Pure peppermint. It must have been some kind of perfume or oil she used. It didn't matter. I loved it as soon as I smelled it.

"I know you wanted to protect me," I said, "and I know why you did what you did, but you have no idea how happy I am to be here with you. Before I met Mathias, I thought you threw me away like trash, but when I learned the truth, I wanted nothing more than for you to be alive, so that I could meet you. And here you are."

Elisabeth pulled away and stepped back. "I shouldn't be surprised that you've met Mathias."

I smiled. "It wasn't the greatest time in my life. We both did things to each other that we regret. And he lied to me about the initiation. I know if I had never been initiated then Lucinda would be powerless."

Again, Elisabeth shook her head. "She would have found another way. She always finds a way."

"Your plan worked though," I said. "It worked for eighteen years."

A smile lit up Elisabeth's face. "Eighteen years. I was so excited when I found out that there was a couple looking to adopt, and they seemed like lovely people. And I'm sorry about what happened to them."

I knew she knew. I knew she had to be the one warning about me about what was to come, what was to happen.

"I'm sorry," she said, and pulled me into her again. We stood like that for a few moments, holding on to each other. I wanted it to last forever, but I knew it couldn't. I needed to move this along though, so I pulled away. I was about to refer to her as my mother, but then I called her by her name instead.

"Elisabeth," I said, "I'm sure you've heard about San Francisco."

She took my hand and then went still, as if she were in a trance. It took me a moment to realize she was watching the past events from my life. She had the same power I had only recently been acquiring.

"I saw bits and pieces just now," she said, releasing my hand. "Lucinda."

I nodded. "It was part of her plan. I have to fix this. I need to get into the original Headquarters. I need to reverse time. Elijah told me that it was possible there. He—" I stopped, unsure how to tell her about Elijah's death.

She looked at me sadly. "I saw it in your mind and it is something I will have to process. I didn't know until now. I never had the connection with him that I had with my sister. He helped me in a way I'll never be able to forget, and then I never saw him again."

"I'm sorry," I said, "but can you help me?"

"I will do whatever I can," Elisabeth said, "but turning back time won't solve anything for you."

"What do you mean?"

"She will just find another way."

I shook my head in frustration. "Then we will have to—to kill her." It was difficult for me to say it out loud, I knew it would have to be done, but it was still difficult. "But not until we get into the Headquarters. She told me she sealed it off, and only she can open it, otherwise I would have done it already. I'm prepared to do it."

Elisabeth nodded. "That doesn't surprise me. There are three options to stop this prophecy from being fulfilled, and this must be done before time is reversed. As long as all of the requirements haven't been fulfilled, the prophecy can be defeated by you or your sister dying, Lucinda dying, or by waiting it out entirely until your birthday. If she doesn't fulfill it before midnight on your nineteenth birthday, it can never be fulfilled."

"And how do you know she hasn't fulfilled all of the requirements?" I asked her.

"Well, the first is killing a Timekeeper."

I turned away in frustration.

"Have you done that, Abigail? I briefly saw something on the Tower Bridge in London."

Tears welled up in my eyes. I turned back around to face her. "I didn't do it on purpose. It was Bessie Watson. She would have killed us all. I let her hand go. She fell to her death from the Tower Bridge in London."

Elisabeth sighed. "It always comes back to that bridge, doesn't it? It doesn't matter. My mother was clever in her plans. She always finds the loophole, but the prophecy is specific. It doesn't matter how you do it, or even if you meant to do it. And I'd say it sounds like you've fulfilled the second requirement, by breaking our most sacred law."

I nodded, wiped the tears from my eyes, and looked up at her. "What's the third requirement?"

"You give up yourself to darkness," Elisabeth said.

I smiled at that. "That's the way out though, isn't it? I would never do that. Ever."

Elisabeth shook her head. "My mother is very manipulative. She'll find a way, trust me. That's one of the reasons she wants you as soon as possible. More time for her to do whatever needs to be done to make that happen."

I paced back and forth across the lecture stage. The tears had dried up now. "Lucinda said they needed this prophecy to come true or else their powers would be gone. What does that mean?"

"The Forbidden Powers," Elisabeth answered. "They will cease to exist. And one of those powers is immortality, so theoretically, if the powers ceased to exist, all those who had used them to remain young would age. Lucinda would die."

"Okay. We need to wait this out then. We need to hide away. If we can hold it out until my birthday, then we'll beat this."

"But the Headquarters will still be sealed," Elisabeth argued, "and my mother will not be there to open it. Remember, she dies if this prophecy isn't fulfilled. And if you don't reverse time, then we're stuck in this dying world."

"Are you saying we're going to have to let her take me?" I asked.

"I don't think there's another way," Elisabeth said. "We have to wait until the last possible moment."

I shook my head. "She won't win though, I'm not going to let myself be given up to evil. I would never let that happen."

Elisabeth stepped forward and put her hands on my arms. "She's already manipulated you once. She'll do it again."

"How do we even know she'll let me into the Headquarters?" I asked. "If she's so worried about this prophecy, wouldn't that be the last place she'd take me?"

"No," Elisabeth said, "she'll take you there. That place is sacred to her and that is where she'll want to be to finally fulfill the prophecy. I know it deep down, she'll be there."

"Alright, then," I said, "we'll wait until there is just enough time left, she'll let us in, and I will somehow avoid her temptations to become—" I struggled to say the word "—evil."

Elisabeth pulled away from me and walked away in frustration.

"What is it?" I asked. Something else was wrong.

She turned around, tears in her eyes, but simply pulled me into another hug.

"It's nothing," she said. "I'm just so grateful to have you back."

I had no idea how and knew it wasn't because of this new ability I inherited, but I could tell she was lying.

"You were able to see what has happened to me," I said. "Well, I've started to feel things when I touch people. Do you know why?"

She pulled away, nodding. "You're an empath. Original Timekeepers have more abilities than a regular Timekeeper. You are able to know what people are feeling, but also to see events that have already happened in their lives, simply by touching them."

"But why can't I see yours?" I asked.

She smiled. "I've become very practiced in not allowing myself to be vulnerable to others. Preparing for the inevitable reunion with my mother I suppose."

The sound of the door to the lecture hall opening pulled us both out of our concentrations on each other. I looked up and saw Henry looking in the room. Elisabeth went rigid.

"Henry?"

Henry smiled. "It's been a while. I hope you'll forgive me for revealing your location. I'm sorry to interrupt, but we shouldn't stay in one location too long. Abigail, do you know what the plan is now?"

I looked at Elisabeth. "We need to go to the Eiffel Tower first, but do you have a place we can meet you?"

"Of course," she said, still a bit teary.

She turned around, reached into her bag, and pulled out a piece of paper and pen. She quickly scribbled an address on it and handed it to me.

"I will meet you there," she said, looking between Henry and me.

Henry nodded. "Very well. Let's go."

Elisabeth quickly gathered her things and together we made our way up the stairs and out of the lecture hall, and out into the world, together again as mother and daughter, for the second time in our lives.

Thomas and Oliver made their way to the heart of Paris—the Île de la Cité. Perrine Naudé, Thomas' friend from the Paris Headquarters, lived in a small flat at 25 Place Dauphine, a small apartment building over-looking a square. Upon arrival, Thomas reached out and pressed the button to Perrine's apartment, looking up at the building as he did.

"I'm pretty sure she's on the third floor," he said, looking back at the button and then back up at the windows to check.

"*Oui?*" came a girl's voice from the intercom.

Thomas secretly thanked his father for teaching him French and responded.

"*Perrine? C'est Thomas Jane. Comment vas-tu?*"

"Thomas," the woman called Perrine said out of the intercom, "*je vais bien! S'il vous plaît, montez.*"

There was a buzz and the door to the apartment building unlocked. Thomas reached out and pulled it open, stepping aside to allow Oliver to enter first.

"So what exactly were you two saying to each other?" Oliver asked, walking ahead into the building.

"I just asked how she was doing and she said great, come on up."

Thomas began to lead Oliver up the steps toward the third floor.

"Is that all?" Oliver asked, a bit interested now. "Perhaps I should take up a foreign language study."

"Perhaps something other than French?" Thomas suggested, giving his friend a pat on the back. "We could do it together."

Oliver nodded as they stepped onto the third floor landing. As they did, Oliver noticed a young woman with blonde hair poking her head out of the door to the apartment directly in front of them. Upon seeing Thomas, she threw the door open and ran toward him, again speaking in French as she did.

"*Ça fait tellement longtemps!*"

"*En effet il a,*" Thomas responded. "*Peut-on parler en anglais? Mon ami ici ne parle pas français.*"

"Of course," Perrine said, nodding. "And who is your friend?"

Thomas looked at Oliver who was raising his eyebrows, clearly wanting a translation.

"Before that," he said, "she said that it has been a long time and I said that it has and that we should speak in English for you."

"Well, thank you," Oliver said.

Thomas smiled. "Perrine, this is Oliver. I grew up with him in America. And before you ask, he is not a Timekeeper, but I have told him everything."

"Always the rule-breaker," Perrine said. "Please come in."

Perrine beckoned them to follow her into the apartment, closing the door behind them as they did.

"Excuse the mess," she said, running around and picking up various garments. She cleared a spot for them on a cream-colored sofa, which was placed in front of a window looking out over the square below. "Have a seat."

Thomas and Oliver sat, and Perrine pulled a chair in from her kitchen table, placing it in front of them.

"I'm afraid my calling on you today is a bit urgent," Thomas said. "I'm sure you've heard that I'm, shall we say, wanted?"

"You know I've never liked Headrick," Perrine said. "She's always been a bit too much for me. I knew there was something wrong about her. When she announced that you were on the run with that

Jordan girl, I knew she wasn't saying something. She says you are responsible for what happened in San Francisco? That the Jordan girl interfered with a premonition of death? But it doesn't make sense. Why wouldn't death have taken her? Now everyone is buzzing about the original family myth being true. Is it?"

Thomas went into a brief explanation about who Abigail really was and what Headrick was really planning. He also told her Headrick was now a murderer, having killed Abigail's uncle, Elijah Callaghan.

"What are you going to do?" Perrine asked.

"It's a bit too long and complex to explain here," Thomas said. "But I was wondering if you could do us a favor?"

Perrine leaned forward, her face turning into a mischievous grin. "Anything."

"We need you to send a message, discreetly of course, to Abigail's father," Thomas went on. "Mathias works in the Paris Headquarters now. We need you to tell him that Abigail is alive and that she is here in Paris. And we kind of need you to do this now. We figured maybe you could go now, bring him out with you, and meet us at the Eiffel Tower?"

Perrine looked at the watch on her wrist. "You caught me before I was about to go in."

"I knew you preferred working nights," Thomas said. "Do you think you can help us out?"

"Of course," Perrine said, nodding. She stood up and walked over to a coatrack by the door, pulling off a large blue coat and putting it on. "Let's get going."

Thomas and Oliver stood and followed her out the door. She

pulled it shut behind them and locked it.

"Meet at the Eiffel Tower in half an hour?" she asked them.

"That works," Thomas said. "Remember, be discreet."

"Got it," Perrine said.

They walked down the stairs and stepped outside of the apartment building, parting ways.

Alma, Henry, and I stood underneath an area by the Eiffel Tower, shaded by trees, and away from the various locals and tourists that were gathered about looking at the historic structure. Alma continued to look around, back and forth, appearing nervous.

"I don't think it's wise to be out in the open like this," she said, looking at me.

"I know, but we won't be too long. We just need to get Mathias and then we can go back to Elisabeth's flat."

"It might have been better if just one of us had come," Henry suggested.

I shook my head. "We need to stick together. I'm still not too fond of the fact that Thomas and Oliver aren't with us."

"They will be soon enough," Alma said, continuing to glance about nervously.

Henry mentioned something about finding a restroom. I protested, but he said he wouldn't be long and it was necessary. He left Alma and I alone, walking away quickly.

"Can I ask you a question?" Alma asked, beginning to hug her arms closely to her. The temperature was starting to drop here as well.

"Of course," I said. "You've always done the same for me."

She smiled, looking up at the Eiffel Tower, and paying particular attention to couples walking to and fro.

"Do you think Oliver and I could have something together?"

I gave her a cheeky grin. "I thought that had already been implied."

A sheepish grin appeared on Alma's face. "Is it that obvious?"

"Yes," I said, nodding. "But you shouldn't be embarrassed. I think you two would be great together."

"I don't know. Sometimes I feel like he doesn't even notice me."

I vividly remember him noticing her when she walked into a room only a few weeks ago. His face had lit up in a way that was unmistakable. That face of someone that was clearly clobbered over someone else.

"He's noticed you," I said. "Trust me."

"Then why won't he ask me on a date or something?"

I looked around us as if it was obvious. "Well, the world is ending. Maybe he put the thought on hold?"

We both giggled at that and she hit me jokingly.

"I understand," she said. "I guess I just thought all of this would bring us closer together. But it hasn't. At least, I don't think it has."

Out of the corner of my eye, I noticed that Henry was walking towards us. I put my hand out and touched Alma's shoulder to comfort her.

"I think it has," I said. "Just give it some time and see. I think something will come of it."

She nodded just as Henry walked up.

"Ah, here they are," he said.

Alma and I turned to see Thomas, Oliver, a girl I didn't recognize, and Mathias heading our way. Mathias was moving faster than the other three, almost sprinting but not running, to get to me. As soon as he did, he threw his arms around me.

"I was so worried," he said into my ear.

We held each other for a moment.

"I know," I said. "But I'm fine. And, Mathias, we found her."

He pulled away from me and the look in his eyes was one I had never seen. It was almost as if, for all the time that I'd known him, he had the smallest spark of life in them, put there by our growing relationship, and now that spark was brighter.

"I don't mean to interrupt," Henry said, "but I don't think it wise for us to spend a minute here any longer. Thomas, is Perrine coming with us?"

I realized Henry was referring to the girl who had arrived with them. Thomas looked at her and smiled, and for the briefest moment, I felt jealously. It was like a sudden burst of heat coursing through my veins. But then it was gone. It was something I'd honestly never felt before. Something I'd accused Phillip of having felt, but never me. And I knew it was something not to dwell on and quickly crushed it. I couldn't allow myself to become vulnerable. Not now.

"Let's go," I said to everyone.

And together, now almost like a small army, a very small army, we made our way to Elisabeth's flat.

CHAPTER SIX

Mathias and Perrine, being the most familiar with Paris, used the address to lead us all back to an apartment building not far from the University that Elisabeth taught at. As I followed Perrine, I noticed she had a confident air about her. She walked through the streets of Paris as if she deserved to be there, as if she had nothing to hide. That spark of jealousy hit me again, but I imagined it was a green balloon in my mind, and I quickly stuck a needle in it and popped it. And it was gone like that.

We turned a corner and found ourselves in front of an old, brick building that went up about seven stories. I stepped in front of Mathias and Perrine and pressed the call button for Elisabeth's apartment.

"Yes?" Elisabeth asked over the intercom.

"It's us," I responded.

"I'll be right down."

A few moments passed before Elizabeth pushed open the large grate door in front of us. As soon as it was open, she caught eyes with Mathias. There was a brief, awkward moment of silence before she beckoned us all to come in. Once inside, she pulled the door shut and began ascending. Her apartment was located on the top floor of the building, at the very end of the hallway. She used a pair of keys to unlock several locks on her door, looking over at me as she did.

"I've become a bit cautious over the years," she said with the hint of a smile. "I always lock up, even if I'm only stepping out." And then she pushed the door open with a bit of a shove. "It always sticks."

I wasn't sure what to expect on the inside, based on the fact that the outside of the building itself didn't look that great, but the inside was quaint. It was clean and everything was up to date as far as kitchen appliances went. It somewhat reminded me of my apartment back at the Chambord Building in San Francisco. And then I remembered. My apartment was now under water.

"Have a seat," Elisabeth said, gesturing toward the open living area behind her.

Once we were all inside, she shut the door, re-locking all of the locks.

"Can we trust her?" I heard Elisabeth ask someone. I assumed she was talking about Perrine, but I was too distracted by the apartment around me. While everyone took a seat, I stayed standing, making my way around the room and looking at all of my mother's possessions. I knew some apartments came with furniture and decor, but I knew within me somehow, that all of this belonged to my mother.

Lining her walls were portraits by various artists, none of them having any kind of meaning or flow, just there to simply celebrate them. She had shelves and shelves of books. Real books. And she had photographs, of her, in various places. There was one I'd already seen. A picture of her in front of the Statue of Liberty in New York City. Another photograph showed her laughing, her hair blowing in the wind, on the edge of a beach. Her feet were barefoot, and she looked happy, genuinely happy. The only thing that was missing were pictures of me. Pictures of my sister. But I knew why those couldn't be there. One particular picture that stood out to me, was a picture of her and Mathias. I picked it up, hoping she wouldn't mind, and lightly touched my fingers over my parents. Did she know how everything would turn out for her? Or was it just as much a surprise as it was to me?

"That was our wedding day," Elisabeth said from behind me. "It may not look like it, as we're not dressed up. We wanted it to be private, secluded. Completely different reasons however. Obviously mine was to keep my mother out of the picture, but Mathias was more for his reclusive nature."

"I'm not reclusive," he said from across the room.

I laughed. It was almost as if they had never been apart.

I placed the picture down and turned to look at her.

"I think I need to know," I said. "Everything. Everything that happened. Before and after."

She reached out and touched my cheek. "I know. And you will. But for now, I think all of you need some rest. Especially our pilots over here. This is a rather large apartment, so let me show you everyone to their rooms, and I promise, we will discuss this tomorrow. Okay?"

I nodded, but there was something that still seemed off. Something was off about this entire meeting with my mother. But I brushed it aside and let her show each of us to a room. Because there were only four, Thomas and I chose to share a room again, and then Henry, Alma, Perrine, and Oliver took the others.

Before I closed the door, I looked back to see Mathias and Elisabeth holding hands and proceeding to what I assumed to be Elisabeth's room. I knew they needed this time, so I closed the door, and brought up my feelings to Thomas.

"Something doesn't feel right," I said, shaking my head.

"What do you mean?" he asked, putting down his bag and pulling out a change of clothes.

"She seems off—Elisabeth. I feel like there's something she's keeping from me."

Thomas began to remove his clothes, and it actually felt comfortable, so I didn't turn around for once.

"I think you are overthinking this," he said, pulling off his shirt. I'd only seen him without his shirt on a couple occasions, so it always gave me a few goosebumps. "You've just met your mother, the woman you've been searching for all this time. You are just feeling a bit overwhelmed."

"I hope," I said.

"Are you sure we can trust this Perrine?" I asked him. "And why is she still here? I thought she had a place here in Paris."

"Her life is in danger now that she's communicated with us and helped us get to Mathias," Thomas said. "I can't risk her being in danger. And I do trust her. She helped me through a lot when I studied here."

He walked over to me and pulled me into him. "I'm not detecting a hint of jealousy, am I?"

Thomas didn't seem angry. On the contrary, he seemed to be enjoying it. I placed my head against his chest, listening to the *thump, thump, thump* of his heartbeat. "Maybe a little."

"You're mine," he said. "And I am yours. Got it?"

I nodded against him, letting his body warm mine. Heat radiated off him and onto me. It was like a fire was brewing between us when we touched. I looked up at him and our eyes met, and then we kissed.

And then before I knew it, he had picked me up, carrying me, continuing to kiss me. He carefully placed me on top of the bed and crawled over me, kissing my neck, my exposed neckline. My hand was over his heart and I could feel it pounding, pounding, pounding against my skin. I closed my eyes and for the briefest moment wanted him to go to that place. That place I'd never been. But I couldn't. Not yet. Not like this.

"We can't go too far," I said, finally allowing myself to let out the breath I didn't realize I was holding.

"Only with what you're comfortable with," he said, continuing to kiss me on my neck, down my arms.

We continued to kiss like that for a bit, until finally he fell to the side of me, pulling me close to him, and we both fell asleep, letting the problems of today be put on hold. They were the problems of tomorrow now. And for now, it was just us.

* * *

The sounds of cars and pedestrians on the streets outside the bedroom window awakened me from my deep sleep the following morning. When I opened my eyes, I was surprised to find that Thomas' arm was no longer wrapped around me. I rolled over to find that he wasn't in the bed.

Sitting up and stretching, I looked around the room. He wasn't there. I sat there for a few minutes, contemplating going back to sleep for a bit longer, and then finally sighed, pushed back the covers, and got out of bed. It had been the best sleep I'd gotten since everything had happened, but there was no more time to rest right. We needed to figure things out.

When I opened the door to the bedroom and stepped out into the hallway, I could hear voices coming from the living room.

"Did you see them?" Thomas was saying.

"No," Oliver said.

"I don't understand," Alma said. "Why would they leave?"

Why would they leave?

My heart pounding, I walked down the hallway and into the living room.

Alma, Oliver, and Thomas were standing in the middle of the room talking. Oliver held an envelope in his hand. Thomas looked pale, as if he had seen a ghost.

"What's going on?" I said aloud.

They all looked over at me and then back at each other. But there was no response. I gestured toward the envelope in Oliver's hand.

"What's that?"

Oliver looked at the envelope as if unsure whether or not to say anything, and then finally held it out to me. I took it.

"Henry, Mathias, and your mother left during the night, Abigail," he said. "They left that. I haven't opened it."

"What do you mean they left?" I asked.

"We checked all the rooms," Alma said. "They aren't here. Oliver got up first and found the envelope."

I looked at it and then back up at Oliver. "And you didn't see them?"

He shook his head. "No, I didn't."

I looked back at the envelope. *For Abigail* was written across the center of it in my mother's handwriting. Sighing, worried about the contents inside, I opened it.

A single letter from my mother was inside. I unfolded it and began to read:

Abigail,

Words cannot describe how thrilled I was to finally meet you again yesterday. I'm glad that you were able to have a happy life with your adoptive parents, and it's clear they were excellent parents.

It saddens me to be writing this now, but I cannot stay here with you. Your connection with your sister grows stronger each day and before long, she will know your location. My location.

Part of my abilities include being able to send you visions in the form of dreams. Before your parents died, I sent you visions, not to warn of their death, but to stay away from the Timekeeping world. Unfortunately, that didn't happen. I again sent you a vision in San Francisco, hoping you would be able to avoid crossing paths with my mother. And while you did everything you could to avoid that, she knew just how to manipulate you, as she did with Ian when he came to lure you into the Timekeeping world.

This is my mistake and I have to fix it. I need you, Abby, to do everything in your power to stay away from Lucinda until your birthday. And I need you to do everything in your power to keep your sister out of your head. Your powers are growing stronger and I've found that the best way to keep a sister out of your head, from experience, is to never think down on yourself and to never need them. When you need them, you open a connection, allowing them into your head. Likewise, when you begin doubting yourself, that leaves you vulnerable and also lets them in. The reason you aren't able to see into Melanie's mind is because she has nothing to feel down about. She has nothing to need you for. Lucinda would have trained her well on not needing those things by stripping her of her humanity. It's part of the prophecy.

The last thing I want to happen is for your sister to die. I know her humanity will return to her if we stop this prophecy from coming true. That means the only way to end it is to end Lucinda. I will do this by meeting her at the original Headquarters. She'll go there sooner or later in hopes you'll end up there too. And that is where I will have the advantage. She doesn't know I'm alive. It's the only card we have to play. And I need to use it, but also keep both you and your sister out of harm's way.

Please tell Thomas Henry is with me. He's agreed to help me in this. Together, we will be there when Lucinda opens the Headquarters, we will end her, and then we will reverse Time.

I know you want to know everything Abigail. Which is why I wrote it all down. I've been writing it all down for years. On my bookshelf, you'll find a leather-bound book with no writing on the spine. Find it and read it. For everything that comes after your birth, read the letters Henry gave you.

I wanted so much to be able to tell you everything, but at least you'll have this.

Please, keep yourself in my apartment until you figure out a way to get out of Paris. They already know you are in the city. I've used my ability to send visions to you to keep myself out of your mind whenever your sister looked in. You are stronger now that we've met, and I know you'll be able to keep her out now without my help, but your best chance of ending this prophecy is to get as far away from them as you can get.

I love you, Mathias loves you, and please tell Thomas his father loves him as well.

Love,

E.

My hands were shaking as I folded up the letter and looked back at the three of them, standing there, watching me. I felt like everything was falling apart.

"She's gone," I said. "They're all gone."

I handed them the letter to let them read it on their own and then went to exactly where my mother told me to go. I couldn't let myself feel down about this, as she had said. She was doing this to protect me. She wasn't running away from me. But even though the world was falling apart around us, I had looked forward to getting to know her, even if it was amongst all of these terrible things happening. But now that was out of the question. She was there, briefly, and then she was gone.

I found the diary exactly where she said it would be. I carefully pulled it off the shelf, worried that I would somehow damage it, and skimmed through the pages. My mother's familiar writing, from the various letters I had read from her, appeared on the pages. Her script was more elegant than the letters I had read, as if she had taken the time to carefully write each and every letter on the page. This was the story. All of it. All of the answers I needed to know were finally here.

A hand touched my shoulder and I turned around quickly. Thomas stood behind me.

"Are you alright?" he asked.

I nodded and looked back at the diary.

"I just need to be alone for a bit," I said.

"Okay, but just know I'm here for you."

I nodded, and then noticed how pale he still was. I had assumed it had been from the knowledge from earlier, but maybe there was something else bothering him. I made a mental note to ask him about it later.

He kissed the top of my forehead and left me alone. With the diary clutched carefully at my side, I walked back to the room Elisabeth had let Thomas and I use and shut the door behind me. The room had a little nook underneath the window which I went over to and curled up in. Then, I opened the diary to the first page. I took several deep breaths to prepare myself and looked down at the first words along the top of the page.

A a *tap, tap, tap* made me look up from the diary. And there it was again. That same gray-brown bird, tapping away at the window. What did it want from me? Why did I feel I had seen it before?

I shrugged it off and looked back down at the first words written on the page.

October 1904.

And then I began to read.

Part Two

Truth
October 1904 to December 1925

CHAPTER SEVEN

October 1904

A piercing scream filled the halls as Abigail Halstead made her way back to the birthing room where Lucinda Callaghan was giving birth to her twins. Lucinda knew it would be twins and had told Abigail so. She had had a premonition. She had seen the two girls being born. And they would have brown hair, just like their father. Abigail didn't have the gift of the sight that Lucinda had. Her family had simply been serving the Callaghan family for as long as she could remember. And Abigail knew Lucinda was evil. She had never aged in the time since Abigail had been born. She had never gotten a wrinkle or even the hint of a grey hair. The woman was unnatural.

Now, as Abigail carried the boiling hot water and several rags, she feared for the lives of the twins Lucinda would be birthing. She knew the woman had no room in her heart for children. She had always been obsessed with power. And she knew there was a reason as to why Lucinda was so obsessed with having twins, but Lucinda had never shared why.

Abigail pushed open the double doors to Lucinda's room with her shoulder and stepped in. The room was dimly lit by candlelight and Lucinda lay in the middle of it on the birthing table. On either side of her were her husband, Richard, and the doctor. Lucinda couldn't remember his last name, but she was almost certain it started with an A.

"Where have you been?" Lucinda spat.

"I was simply getting everything you asked, ma'am," Abigail replied.

"Just set everything down there," said Richard.

"That will be all, Miss," the doctor said curtly.

Abigail gave a quick curtsy, a requirement of Lucinda's, and exited the room. Then she sat outside, as she had been instructed to, and waited. There were more piercing screams from Lucinda. It seemed to go on forever, until, finally, she heard the cry of a baby. Abigail loved children, and so for the first time in a very long time, her heart felt warm and happy. And then she heard the second cry. Twins, just as Lucinda had told her it would be.

Abigail smiled to herself and happily conjured the thoughts of spending time with the children. She knew there would be lots of memories, as there was no way Lucinda would even consider changing a child's diaper. But then something happened that dissolved her thoughts. A third cry. And then, utter, horrid screaming. She stood up and entered the room.

"NO!"

"Honey," Richard was saying, "sweetheart, it's okay."

Lucinda pushed herself up, grabbed a scalpel, and stuck it into her husband's neck. A sane, rational person would have been utterly horrified at the sight. That is, the sight of Lucinda ramming the scalpel into Richard, the sight of him being utterly caught by surprise, and the sight of blood spewing forth from his neck until, finally, he fell to the floor dead in a pool of his own blood.

Abigail Halstead was a sane, rational person. But she had been around Lucinda Callaghan for a long time. And this was nothing new. Richard had actually not been Lucinda's first husband. Knowing how old she was, Abigail had no idea how many husbands she had had. Her previous husband had suffered an injury not long after they were married, leaving him unable to produce a child. Lucinda had ended the marriage not long after that by slicing his throat during the night. She was evil. Pure evil. And Abigail feared daily that the children might also be.

"What is the problem, Miss?" Abigail asked.

Lucinda turned her attention from her dead husband to Abigail.

"The problem," she spat, "is that there are three of them. There were only supposed to be two. And to top it off, they all have blonde hair."

Abigail turned her attention to the crib where children had been placed, and sure enough there were three, two girls, one boy, and each of them had blonde hair; not the brown Lucinda had foreseen.

"Lucy," the doctor said, "you need to lie back. You're going to overdo it."

Lucinda did as she was instructed. For some reason, this doctor seemed to be the only man she would listen to.

"What are we going to do, Aldridge?" Lucinda asked. "Do you think drowning the boy would do it?"

Abigail's heart almost stopped. She had become almost immune to watching Lucinda kill her parents and her husbands. But watching her kill children? Abigail didn't know if she could bear it.

"I don't think that would work," Aldridge responded. "Considering the twins you saw had brown hair, I think it means these aren't the children we've been waiting for. Besides, the boy could be put to good use later on."

"Then kill them all," Lucinda said. "What's the point? We will try again."

"Perhaps," Aldridge said, but then he stopped. He looked as if an idea was coming to him.

"What is it?" Lucinda asked.

"Perhaps," he continued, "the children you saw were the children of one of these babies. Your grandchildren."

Lucinda sat up again. "You're a genius."

The babies started crying and Lucinda turned an icy stare to Abigail. "Why are you just standing there? Take care of them and take them away for a while. I need rest."

Abigail did as she was told, doing her best to scoop up the three babies and take them away from the evil they had been born into.

Elisabeth Callaghan first realized her mother was unlike most mothers in the small village of Dingle, Ireland when she was seven years old. It was around that time that young Elisabeth first came to the realization that not everyone was the same; everyone was different. Her mother was no exception.

Lucinda Callaghan had always been cool, calculated, and somewhat on guard. She was ready to strike whenever necessary, about what though, Elisabeth didn't know. The one thing Elisabeth was positive about, however, was she was her mother's favorite. There was simply no question about it. Her sister, Eleanor, had always been disobedient, and their mother seemed to hate Elijah no matter what he did. But Elisabeth did everything her mother asked of her, and as soon as she was able to comprehend things, her mother began training her to be a Timekeeper, something she also attempted with Eleanor, who never cared for the ancestral gift she had inherited.

Instead, Eleanor found solace in attending St. Mary's Church in the little village of Dingle near their family's Headquarters, where they had grown up. Eleanor would spend her days praying in the church, as well as spend time with those that attended there and tell them stories about why her family wasn't good and why she didn't want to be a part of it. Of course, she knew never to mention what it was her family did, for she didn't want to come off as insane. And it was at St. Mary's that the clergy and parishioners comforted her and welcomed her into their family.

Lucinda was infuriated when she found out about Eleanor's attending church. Even though she had long ago given up on the idea of her daughter following in her footsteps, she still adamantly disagreed with the idea of spending time at the church. Lucinda believed Timekeepers were above all, including religions.

A fight broke out between mother and daughter worse than

anything that had occurred in the Callaghan Headquarters. Lucinda destroyed all of her daughters blessed crucifixes, leaving them in shambles on the floor. When Elisabeth found Eleanor, face down in her bed in tears, she didn't feel the least bit sorry for her.

"You deserved it," Elisabeth said, leaning against the wall of Eleanor's room. "Mother has always given you the opportunity to follow in the family's footsteps. And at every turn, you've refused her offering."

Eleanor looked up at Elisabeth, her eyes filled to the brim with tears. "Do you really think what she is trying to turn you into is good? It isn't. She's trying to fulfill some evil prophecy. I heard her telling Aldridge about it. And to top it off, she's never even loved Elijah. She's never offered him anything. Do you really think she loves us? Truly?"

"Of course she loves us," Elisabeth spat back, rolling her eyes. "You're pathetic."

"Back off, Elisabeth," Elijah spat, walking through the door and pushing against Elisabeth as he did. He walked over to the edge of Eleanor's bed and knelt down, putting a hand on her back to comfort her.

"You two are ridiculous," Elisabeth said, leaving the room.

"Mother has turned her against us," Eleanor said, continuing to cry softly into her bed sheets.

"She'll come around," Elijah said.

Eleanor rolled over onto her back. "I can't do this anymore. Elijah, I need to go. Tonight."

Elijah looked worried. He wouldn't mind leaving. He knew his mother would never feel the same way about him that she felt about Elisabeth. But he would have to leave Abigail. And he loved Elisabeth and knew that he couldn't leave her in a toxic relationship with his mother. But he also realized Eleanor had had enough. She needed to get away.

"I think I have to stay," Elijah said, "for Elisabeth, and Abigail. But you know I'll help you do whatever it is you need to do. Just say the word."

Eleanor nodded and brushed the tears from her eyes. "I've talked to a few of the nuns at St. Mary's and they said they could get me to London. I want to be a part of the church forever. I want to become a nun."

Elijah smiled. His sister's faith was something that reminded him there was hope after all. "Let's do it."

That night, Elijah helped Eleanor escape her mother's wrath forever.

Four Years Later

Eleanor had been fourteen when Elijah helped her sneak out in the middle of the night. Lucinda was furious the next morning. She ransacked Eleanor's room, destroying all of her daughter's possessions. She didn't plan to look for Eleanor. As far as she was concerned, the girl was dead. So life moved on at the Callaghan Headquarters. Elijah continued his studies in the village, and Elisabeth continued working closely with her mother, refusing to believe what Eleanor had told her the night she left. Elisabeth knew that while her mother was different from the other mothers, she was capable of love. She had to be. Why else would Elisabeth be her favorite? She refused to believe there was any kind of prophecy Lucinda was trying to fulfill.

December 1922

"You'll be moving to London this week."

Elisabeth looked up in confusion at her mother's sudden declaration. She had no idea why she was suddenly moving to London.

"Pardon?"

Lucinda looked at her daughter from her office desk, and then stood up, taking off her black spectacles and placing them on the desk. She walked over to her daughter, her heels clicking against the floor, and placed both her hands on her daughter's shoulders.

"It's time for you to find a husband, my love."

Elisabeth recoiled at the idea. She had never been courted by anyone, let alone courted anyone herself. Why was her mother suddenly asking this of her?

"But I don't want to find a husband," Elisabeth replied. "I want to stay here with you."

Lucinda's face turned ugly. "You will do as I say."

Elisabeth looked away, confused at her mother's sudden, agitated behavior. Then she felt her mother's hands on her cheek, turning her face back to her.

"I'm sorry, sweetheart," Lucinda said. "I didn't mean to lash out like that. It's just time. You're eighteen. You need to think about starting a family of your own."

Elisabeth had always been in the business of making her mother happy. So, instead of arguing again, she agreed. Her mother helped her pack her things, continued to reiterate the fact that it was important to follow her instructions to the "T", and then Aldridge and Lucinda were taking Elisabeth down to the Dingle, Ireland Port to ship off for London. She hadn't even said goodbye to Elijah. They hadn't spoken much since Eleanor left. That day, he simply watched her go from the end of the long hallway that led out of their Headquarters. And she didn't look back.

CHAPTER EIGHT

December 1922

Elisabeth Callaghan stood outside of the Old Bailey, gazing up at
the statue of Lady Justice. The statue exemplified the pursuit of
justice in a society that was constantly being tested. In one hand,
Lady Justice carried the sword, signifying that justice is prompt and
final, and in the other hand, her balance scales, signifying the
weighing of any evidence given at trial. But what Elisabeth found
most ironic, especially considering the statue was on the building of a
courthouse, was the fact that Lady Justice was missing her famous
blindfold. The blindfold was meant to represent Lady Justice not
being biased. And Elisabeth found it even more ironic considering
the trial currently taking place, and the outcome, which she had
already foreseen, that would follow.

As Elisabeth made her way into the building, she let her fingers
trace its walls. She felt the pain and sorrow that had passed through

them, and the pain and sorrow yet to come. Elisabeth's power to feel the past, as well as the future, came to her almost a year after her eighteenth birthday. It was one of many individual powers that could only be bestowed on original Timekeepers. Each Timekeeper received a different power. A power that, while sometimes beneficial, could at other times become a great curse.

Flashes of a great war, one greater and more dangerous than its predecessor, flashed through Elisabeth's mind as she made her way up the stairs, toward the entrance of the building. She saw images of aircraft flying over London, dropping bombs on the buildings. She saw destruction, pain, and suffering. It came to her in quick, short bursts, and it caused her so much agony she had to stop and pull her hand from the wall, clutching at her chest and taking slow, deep breaths.

"Are you alright, Miss?"

Elisabeth looked up into the eyes of a young policeman. He was leaning in close and peering at her. She quickly smiled and nodded.

"I'm fine, thank you."

She brushed past him and made her way into the building in hopes of finding a seat in the courtroom. She had made sure to arrive early, knowing full well the trial had been quite publicized, and the public would soon be arriving to see what would happen. Elisabeth had foreseen what would happen as soon as she had arrived in London, and while she was appalled at the idea that the woman on trial wouldn't be receiving justice, she really didn't think it necessary to be here. It was her mother who had demanded she come.

The courtroom was nearly full when Elisabeth entered, but she saw a seat near a man, who appeared to be a little older than her, with dirty blond hair. She approached him and asked if the seat next to him was taken. He shook his head and she took her seat, looking around the room at all of the people. She had no idea what her mother was expecting her to find here, other than an innocent woman being put on trial. The man next to her appeared not to be too interested in the proceedings either. He too was looking around the room, as if in search of someone.

It was then that she saw him. He was sitting down on the lowest level of the court room, sitting next to a man he looked unhappy to be with. And he looked unhappy to be here. It was what drew him to her attention. He looked as if he wanted to dash out of the room as quickly as he could. He looked as if he couldn't handle being around anyone, let alone a room with hundreds of people in it. His hair was brown, cut short. He had no facial hair, easily revealing his chiseled facial features. He was handsome, very handsome.

Elisabeth could feel the man next to her reposition in his seat. She inclined her head to look at him out of the corner of her eye and noticed he too had been drawn to the man at the lowest level.

"Mathias," the man next to her muttered.

Elisabeth turned completely to face the man and gave him a questioning look.

"I'm sorry," she said, "did you say something?"

She could tell he hadn't meant to say it out loud, but he had outed himself nonetheless.

"I'm just talking to myself," he said, a smile appearing on his face. He had an American accent. He held out his hand. "Henry Jane.

Quite the circus show this trial is turning into, isn't it? All of these people here just to catch a glimpse of this woman and her lover."

There was a brief hesitation as Elisabeth wondered if she should shake the man's hand, knowing what would happen if she did. She let a moment pass and then took it.

Flashes.

They passed before her eyes quickly. She saw the man, Henry, holding a baby. And she saw a woman, also holding the baby. But she couldn't quite make out the woman's face. And she also saw the man who had attracted her attention in the courtroom.

"It is quite interesting to say the least," Elisabeth agreed, releasing his hand and looking back toward the front of the courtroom.

"And your name?"

She tensed. She should have known he would ask this. It wasn't that she cared giving out her name, but more so that her mother warned her against doing so.

"Elisabeth James," she said. The family surname needed to be protected. *Always*. It was what her mother always told her.

"Pleasure," Henry replied. He sat back in his chair and returned his gaze to the man at the front of the room, the one he had called Mathias. Elisabeth had a feeling Henry was here because of the woman holding the baby in her vision whom she couldn't see. There was something going on between Mathias and Henry, and it also involved her. From what she had seen, she could the woman and Henry had had a child together. Elisabeth always tried to not let other people's business consume her, but this was hard to do when it was thrown upon her so quickly.

The next hour passed slowly. Much of the time was spent deliberating on whether or not certain letters between the woman on trial and her lover could be admitted to the jury as evidence. Already knowing the outcome of the trial, Elisabeth sat in her seat wondering why her mother had wanted her to come here. Had she wanted her to meet the man Elisabeth had been drawn to at the front of the courtroom? Perhaps she had wanted Elisabeth to meet the man sitting next to her? She had no idea.

A recess was declared and many individuals began moving toward the lobby to stretch their legs. Mathias began to do so, and Elisabeth allowed herself to follow him. She noticed Henry was not far behind her. It was when he actually brushed past her and walked quickly up to Mathias that she sensed a scene was about to break out. She casually moved out of the line of fire but stayed near enough to eavesdrop on the potential quarrel.

"Mathias," the man spat, moving toward him.

Mathias, who had been standing with his back facing Henry and standing beside the older man, turned and looked at Henry with first surprise and then pure rage.

"Henry," he said, the disgust evident in his voice, "did you follow me here?"

"Of course, I followed you here," Henry said. "My child needs a mother. How could you allow Bessie to abandon her own son? You should be ashamed of yourself. Taking off with another man's wife. Ripping a mother away from her child."

The man's face turned beet red, and the man who stood next to him, which Elisabeth assumed to be his father based on their similar physical features, stepped in.

"I don't know what business you have with my son, sir," the man said, "but I will not allow you to make a mockery of us in front of all of these people. You need to leave. Now."

The quarrel was starting to attract the attention of others and it even looked as if some officers were about to step in. Henry held up his hands in defeat, shaking his head, but before he walked away, he said, "She needs help, Mathias. Help that neither of us can give her."

As Henry walked away, Mathias glared daggers at him before walking away with his father.

As much as Elisabeth wanted to follow Mathias, she felt a need to comfort Henry. He looked distraught, and she felt for him. Having grown up away from most of the world, she suddenly felt a longing to help another person. And so she followed him instead.

"Sir. Sir!"

Elisabeth was running after Henry, down the steps of the Old Bailey. But he wasn't turning around.

"Mr. Jane."

That got his attention. Henry stopped and turned around, looking at Elisabeth in confusion, and then quickly recognizing her from the courtroom.

"Yes, Miss?"

Elisabeth slowed her pace now as she walked toward Henry, her heart racing after running to keep up with him. As she approached him, she realized he was quite handsome. He didn't draw her attention as much Mathias had, but there was something attractive about him.

"I'm sorry to have eavesdropped," Elisabeth said, "but I couldn't help overhearing the quarrel between you and that man back there. I, well, I suppose I just wanted to make sure you were okay."

The man raised his eyebrow in surprise and then looked down at his feet, shuffling them. He didn't say anything for a moment, and the two of them stood there awkwardly in the cold December weather.

"Thank you," he finally said. "That's not something most people would do."

A smile lit up Elisabeth's face. "I'd like to think I'm not like most people."

"Perhaps not," he responded. He brought his hand up and tugged at his beard for a moment before he finally said, "Would you like to have a coffee with me?"

The question took her by surprise, but she nodded her head. He smiled and led her in the direction of a coffeehouse.

Henry and Elisabeth sat in a coffeehouse not too far from the Old Bailey. They had both ordered a coffee and were waiting patiently. Elisabeth, not knowing what to say, was spending the majority of the time looking out of the window they had been seated next to and admiring the passersby of London as they walked to and fro, going about their everyday lives.

Henry sat across from her and was moving his leg up and down, up and down in a constant motion and finally Elisabeth lightly tapped him with the heel of her shoe.

"You're shaking the whole table."

His leg stopped and a blush erupted in his face.

"Sorry."

She smiled. "It's okay. Do you want to talk about what happened back there? It's fine if you don't, but I figured it's probably important to talk about tense situations once in a while."

Henry sighed, also beginning to look out the window. He didn't say anything, so Elisabeth didn't press him. A waitress came and deposited two coffees and a cup of cream onto their table and walked away. Elisabeth picked up her cup and sipped while Henry began adding cream. She noticed he added quite a bit. He looked up, realizing she was watching him and stopped.

"Sorry," he said, "did you want some? Black coffee has always been too bitter for me."

Elisabeth shook her head and took another sip of hers. Henry began stirring the cream into his coffee, but didn't take a sip. Finally, he sighed and then spoke.

"The man that you saw me quarreling with back there," he said, "was Mathias Benedict. I met him in America and he took a fancy to my wife, Bessie."

Elisabeth knew this was most likely the case based on what she had already seen, but she had hoped it would be something different. She didn't quite like hearing the man she had taken an interest in was also engaged in an affair with another man's wife. Regardless, she didn't speak up and let Henry continue with his story.

"At first I thought Bessie wasn't interested in him. She was carrying our child and we were doing well. However, that all changed after

Thomas was born. She didn't want to have anything to do with our son. I've heard stories in the field. You see it has always been my intention to go into medicine and I've heard that women after childbirth can sometimes be unaccepting of their child, but they soon come around. I figured this was the case with Bessie.

"But then I found out in the worst of all ways. I stumbled upon them engaged in, well, pardon me, but engaged in relations of an intimate nature. I knew then she didn't desire me. She had no interest in raising our child. And then one day they were gone. I guess I'm here to try and win her back. Our child needs a mother, you see? How can I possibly raise him on my own?"

A tear had appeared at the edge of Henry's eye, but he wiped it away and finally took a sip from his coffee.

"Forgive me," Elisabeth said, "but you mentioned that Bessie needed help. How so?"

Henry sat down his cup. "She's always been delicate. She didn't have the greatest relationship with her mother, and it affected her greatly. Before she left, she had begun to act a bit strangely. For example, I once found her talking to herself, completely alone in a room. At other times, she claimed she had been hearing voices. And her temper, she had a violent temper. At first, the things she said to me were merely threatening, but towards the end, they were worse. The night she left, she slashed at me at with a knife."

Henry pulled up the sleeve of his left arm and showed Elisabeth a wound. It was healing, but it was still ugly.

"This might be a bit forward," Elisabeth said, "but do you think she is safe to be around your child?"

It Henry's eyes filled with tears. He shook his head.

"I don't know. I just don't want my child to grow up without a mother. Does Bessie need help? Yes. She does. But I still have feelings for her. I have a child with her for Christ's sake. Forgive me." He began taking deep breaths.

"It's okay," Elisabeth said. "It's understandable that you would feel this way."

Henry picked up a napkin and wiped his eyes. He then set it down and looked at Elisabeth.

"I noticed the way you looked at him."

Elisabeth's heart skipped a beat. "Excuse me?"

"Mathias Benedict," he responded. "The man that I argued with. You were watching him, very closely."

In response to his forwardness, Elisabeth attempted to smile. "I'm not sure what you're implying, sir."

"There's no need denying it," Henry said. "I saw that same look in my wife's eyes. Will you help me?"

She gulped at his question. *Help him.*

"How could I possibly help you?"

"You're a beautiful woman," he responded. "You seem kind, honest, and knowledgeable. You could make him fall for you. And it would be genuine. Whatever he has with Bessie, it isn't genuine. I don't even know if it's genuine with me. I'm starting to believe Bessie is in it for the desire, the lust. I've known Mathias. She is manipulating him, just like she manipulated me, only I have to keep living with it, because of the life we created. You could help me. You could get him to leave her."

Elisabeth was finding it difficult to process what Henry was asking of her. It felt wrong. She didn't know this woman. She didn't know if Henry was being honest. Yes, she had seen bits and pieces in his memories, but she couldn't be sure.

"That seems like quite a terrible thing to do," she said. "I don't even know Bessie. I don't even know if what you're telling me is true."

"Forget about her," Henry said. "Remove her from the equation. You were entranced by him, not her. Were you really going to let something like that stop you?"

He seemed enraged now, as if he wasn't thinking sensibly about what he was saying.

"And you don't need to know what she looks like," he continued, "in fact, you should try to stay away from her as much as possible. I told you about her temper. The less she knows about you, the better. We can work out the details later. I can get her to meet with me, and while I am doing that, you can court Mathias."

She shook her head at that and laughed. "This is ridiculous. Do you realize how ridiculous this sounds?" Is this what her mother had seen? Had her mother wanted her to get involved in a relationship with Mathias? Elisabeth wouldn't put it past her mother to want her to carry through some scheme to get a man to end his relationship with another woman. Lucinda would find a great pleasure in such an act.

"Please," Henry begged her. "I know this sounds ludicrous, but please. Please help me."

Elisabeth looked away for a moment, out through the window

watching as people walked to their various destinations. Leave it up to her mother to get involved in all of this. She was sure Lucinda probably found some kind of humor in it all. Elisabeth still had the strong, yearning desire to please her mother, and that man, Mathias —she wanted to know him. Finally, after taking a deep breath, she turned back to Henry.

"Very well."

Henry's face lit up in a smile. "Thank you."

He held out his hand. Elisabeth hesitated to shake it, not knowing what she might see, but she took it. She saw flashes again. This time she saw this man marrying Bessie, Bessie who was a Timekeeper. She saw this man being initiated as a Timekeeper. And in it all, she saw Mathias. He had gone to San Francisco to train under Bessie's father, and he had fallen for the girl, even though she was married. But the strange thing was, she couldn't make out Bessie's face. She knew it was Bessie, but she couldn't see her.

Elisabeth pulled her hand away and placed it in her lap. Everything made sense now. Of course her mother would want her to find a Timekeeper to marry. But why couldn't she see this man's wife?

"So," she said, looking Henry in the eye, "where do we begin?"

"I've found that Mathias is a bit reclusive."

Henry and Elisabeth were sitting in Henry's flat. It had been a few days since they first met at the Old Bailey. Elisabeth had agreed to meet Henry to hash out their plan. A part of her felt guilty about what she was doing, but at the time same time, she remembered what her mother had said about Bessie and felt somewhat justified.

"Won't that make things difficult?" Elisabeth asked.

"Possibly," Henry responded, "but I think I can persuade him to meet me under the guise that it will be the final time and you can be there. That will probably be our best opportunity. Otherwise, you may never get the chance."

"Why is he reclusive?" Elisabeth asked.

Henry took a sip from the teacup in front of him.

"From what I've gathered, his mother was murdered when he was young. It happened out in the streets, so Mathias' father instilled in him this idea that the world would always be dangerous. He never let his son go explore it."

Elisabeth nodded in understanding. "When did you want to meet him?"

"I asked him to meet me at St. Patrick's Church in Soho Square."

"You want to meet him at a church?" Elisabeth asked, puzzled by the strange choice of location.

Henry shrugged. "I figured it would be the least likely place for a commotion to break out. Plus, it's just down the street from me."

Elisabeth smiled. "It seems you are just being indolent."

Henry shrugged again. "Perhaps, but it is also Sunday and I need to go to church. My plan is to attend mass, which is in half an hour, and he'll be there after that. There are some nice boutiques around that area, so I thought you could look around and wait for mass to let out. Not that anything is open, however, so I hope you enjoy window shopping."

"We're meeting him *today*?" Elisabeth asked, surprised at Henry's quick planning.

"Sooner the better," Henry said. "Is that okay with you?"

She remembered what her mother had said about Bessie. And how she had mentioned to take care of this quickly. As much as she wasn't ready to break up a relationship today, she knew it had to be done. She nodded.

CHAPTER NINE

"I've found that Mathias is a bit reclusive."

Henry and Elisabeth were sitting in Henry's flat. It had been a few days since they first met at the Old Bailey. Elisabeth had agreed to meet Henry to hash out their plan. A part of her felt guilty about what she was doing, but at the time same time, she remembered what her mother had said about Bessie and felt somewhat justified.

"Won't that make things difficult?" Elisabeth asked.

"Possibly," Henry responded, "but I think I can persuade him to meet me under the guise that it will be the final time and you can be there. That will probably be our best opportunity, otherwise, you may never get the chance."

"Why is he reclusive?" Elisabeth asked.

Henry took a sip from the teacup in front of him as he considered this question.

"From what I've gathered, his mother was murdered when he was young. It happened out in the streets, so Mathias' father instilled in him this idea that the world would always be this dangerous and he never let his son go explore it."

Elisabeth nodded in understanding. From what she had seen when she had shook Henry's hand the other day, she knew that Mathias had gone to San Francisco to train, so he at least had gotten away. But that was a requirement of all Timekeepers in training, so his father couldn't necessarily prevent it. And by then, Mathias was most likely reclusive enough that he didn't go out in San Francisco either.

She looked back at Henry. "When did you want to meet him?"

"I asked him to meet me at St. Patrick's Church in Soho Square."

"You want to meet him at a church?" Elisabeth asked, clearly puzzled by the strange choice of location.

Henry shrugged. "I figured it would be the least likely place that a commotion would break out. Hopefully everyone would be neutral. Plus it's just down the street from me."

Elisabeth smiled at him. "It seems you are just being indolent."

Henry shrugged again. "Perhaps, but it is also Sunday and I need to go to church. My plan is to attend mass, which is in half an hour, and then he'll be there after that. There are some nice boutiques around that area, so I thought you could look around and wait for mass to let out. Not that anything is open, however, so I hope you enjoy window shopping."

"We're meeting him *today*?" Elisabeth asked, clearly surprised at Henry's quick planning.

"Sooner the better," Henry said. "Is that okay with you?"

She remembered what her mother had said about Bessie. And how she had mentioned to take care of this quickly. As much as she wasn't ready to break up a relationship today, she knew it had to be done. She nodded.

The tower of St. Patrick's Church in Soho Square loomed in the distance. It was smaller than some of the other churches in London, but Elisabeth was still drawn to its presence. It was majestic in a way.

Mass was just letting out, so throngs of people were exiting the church. Henry was already inside. As instructed, Elisabeth had spent the last hour in the area, browsing. And as Henry had told her, since it was Sunday, not much was open. She stood off in the distance, her hands in her pockets as she gazed at the church. And then she saw him. He was walking across the square, rather quickly, and he looked nervous at being caught in the crowd of people leaving the church. Her instructions from Henry were to follow him in and then take her place at a pew and pretend to be praying. She couldn't believe she was working on breaking up a relationship in a church and thought she might burn up as soon as she entered. But then she remembered she was also trying to save a marriage. Was this a good thing or a bad thing?

She shook the thoughts out of her head and began the short walk across the square to the church. As she walked, a group of nuns were also leaving the church and she accidentally brushed up against one of them. She turned, an apologetic smile on her face.

"My apologies," she said, looking into the eyes of her sister.

Eleanor stood in front of her, wearing a habit, and looking just as shocked as Elisabeth probably looked.

"Lis," Eleanor whispered softly. Eleanor threw her arms around her sister and held her tightly. Elisabeth attempted to return the gesture, still puzzled and surprised at the reunion.

"Sister Bernadette?"

Eleanor pulled away and looked to another nun approaching.

"Who is this?" the nun asked, also smiling and looking at Elisabeth. "I'm going to guess it's your sister, considering you look almost exactly alike, but I'll let you tell me."

Eleanor nodded. "It is. Sister Margaret, this is my twin sister Elisabeth."

Sister Margaret held out her hand. "Pleasure to meet you."

Elisabeth nodded and shook Sister Margaret's hand. For the first time in a long time, the images that flashed before her mind were tranquil. Sister Margaret came from a good family. Her parents had loved her and cared for her. They had supported her vocation in becoming a nun. Elisabeth pulled her hand away.

"Sister Margaret," Eleanor said, "would you give us a minute to catch up? I'll meet up with you and the other sisters."

Sister Margaret nodded, placing a comforting hand on Eleanor's shoulder and smiling as she walked away.

"Bernadette?" Elisabeth asked.

"Nuns take on a different name," Eleanor responded.

Elisabeth nodded and Eleanor waited for Sister Margaret to be out of earshot before she spoke again. "Why are you doing this?"

Elisabeth sighed. She should have known that her sister had embraced her earlier not as a reunion but to touch her and understand what she was doing in London.

"Honor thy father and mother," Elisabeth said.

Eleanor stepped back as if Elisabeth had struck her across the face.

"Thou shalt not kill, Elisabeth," Eleanor spat. "And our mother has done plenty of that."

Elisabeth turned away. She needed to go.

"What you are doing is not right," Eleanor said behind her.

Elisabeth turned back to her. "Who made you the judge? Isn't that the whole idea, Ellie? Let God be the judge. Not you. I've made my choices. And you've made yours. Go live your life. You've clearly been doing just fine without Elijah and I."

Elisabeth turned and walked away, tears pouring down her face. She knew she couldn't do this now. She didn't want to let Henry down, but she couldn't go in that church. Instead, she made her way to a bench in the Soho Square garden and sat down. The tears were coming fast now, and she couldn't do anything except put her face in her hands and let them come.

Mathias Benedict had had enough. He stood in St. Patrick's Church, looking at Henry Jane, who kept looking around as if he was waiting for something.

"I'm sorry, Henry," he said, "I really am. But Bessie made her choice. I didn't pursue her. She pursued me. And I know that doesn't make it right, but we're too far in now."

"She has a *child*, Mathias," Henry cried. "Does that mean anything to you? No, I might not be able to repair what I had with Bessie, but she needs to be there for her child."

"Perhaps, you could bring the child here then?" Mathias suggested. "We could work out some sort of arrangement."

Henry looked as if he had been slapped. "Are you serious? This isn't our home. Bessie isn't from here. Our family is in San Francisco and that is where my son will be staying."

Mathias sighed. "I don't know what you want me to do. I will tell Bessie that the child will be staying in San Francisco and let her decide what to do. But Henry, I can't keep meeting you. This has to stop."

Henry looked around impatiently again.

"Are you looking for something, Henry?"

Henry looked back at Mathias and shook his head. "No, and if we weren't in a church Benedict, I'd say some things to you."

Mathias put his hand up. "I'm done." He turned and began to walk away.

"No, wait!"

Mathias turned around and looked at Henry, waiting to hear why he should wait. Henry simply looked around again, confusion and impatience on his face, and then he sighed as if giving up.

Mathias sighed as well, rolled his eyes, and walked out of the church.

Mathias strolled quickly out of the church and across the street through the Soho Square garden. He felt horrible. Guilty. He had destroyed a marriage and taken a child from his mother. All for what? Sex? Mathias had given Bessie his virginity. He had given her everything. He didn't have the heart to tell Henry that even here in

London Bessie wasn't being faithful. He knew she was going around and being intimate with men throughout the city. She had told him. They didn't even sleep in the same room or make love anymore. The only reason he hadn't told her to leave was because of his father. His father always had high expectations for him and for some reason, he had taken a liking to Bessie. Maybe she'd slept with him too. He laughed aloud at that.

The sounds of a woman crying broke him from his train of thought. He looked to his left and saw a woman, about his age, with beautiful blonde hair that fell down her back. She was sitting forward on the bench, her face in her hands, making no attempt to hide her sobs. Something about her drew him near. He felt a strong urge to comfort her and make her feel safe. It was something he had never felt with anyone, not even Bessie. He sat down on the bench next to her.

"Are you alright?" he asked.

The woman looked up in confusion and then in surprise. Her eyes grew wide and she quickly wiped away her tears.

"I—it's nothing."

"It didn't seem like nothing," Mathias said. "I honestly can't believe I'm over here, but I just felt drawn to you. And that sounded pretty odd. My apologies. I'm Mathias Benedict."

He held out his hand and the woman took it. For a moment, it seemed like she went into a sort of hazy, dreamlike state, but then she was fine again.

"Elisabeth Callaghan," the woman responded, pulling her hand away. It was the one rule her mother had given her—not to use their last name. But she suddenly didn't care.

"Pleasure to meet you, Elisabeth," Mathias said. "Well, I need to get going. I just wanted to make sure you were alright."

Mathias stood up to leave, smiled, and began to walk away.

"Wait," Elisabeth said.

Mathias turned around and looked at her.

"This might sound odd, but will you sit with me?"

Mathias tensed. He'd already been out long enough that day and the world felt like it was closing in on him. He longed for the emptiness of his bedroom back at the London Headquarters.

"I really must be going," he said.

The woman had a pained, almost pleading look on her face. "*Please.*"

Mathias looked away for a moment, thinking it over, and decided for once he needed to do something for someone else.

"Very well," he said, walking back to the bench and taking his seat next to Elisabeth.

The two of them sat there awkwardly for a few minutes before Elisabeth finally spoke up.

"I'm just going to be honest with you," she said. "I saw you the other day at the Old Bailey with your father, and I was drawn to you. And then I met Henry Jane and he told me about your relationship with his wife, and we concocted a plan for you to fall for me and leave her. And I'm telling you because I really do feel something for you and if that turns into something, I don't want it to start with a lie."

Mathias just sat there, listening, as this woman poured everything out to him. He couldn't believe Henry had done this, but he realized he didn't care. He had felt drawn to this woman too, and if they both felt this way, then surely that meant something.

"Please say something," Elisabeth said. "I can't stand this silence."

"I feel the same way," he said. And then he found himself revealing everything to this woman he had only just met. He told her about the murder of his mother, his relationship with his father, and how he didn't feel anything for Bessie but simply wanted to make his father happy. And in that moment, something new started.

That evening, Elisabeth laid in her bed, staring up at the ceiling, thinking of the events that had transpired that day. Mathias and Elisabeth had made plans to meet again, and immediately afterward, they went back to the church together and found Henry. Needless to say, he was surprised, but agreed to allow Mathias to find the time to call it off with Bessie. In the meantime, he would return to San Francisco in hopes Bessie would follow soon after.

Elisabeth kept thinking about how she felt she had done the right thing for once. But she also thought about her mother. She knew that she had to come to the realization that her mother was not a good person. And she also had to come to terms that there was something much more sinister going on than she had previously believed. And she knew the only person who would have the answers was Eleanor. She left all those years ago because she found something out. Elisabeth remembered her mentioning an evil prophecy their mother was trying to fulfill. At the time, Elisabeth had put the idea out of her mind. However, very recently, she had begun to think Eleanor was telling the truth. Her mother had suddenly wanted her to come to London to find a husband, and she had had very specific instructions about where to go and where to be. She knew it was time to cut ties with her mother, but she had to know from Eleanor what the prophecy was.

And so, for the first time in years, she tried to speak to her sister telepathically.

"Ellie?" she said in her mind. *"Are you there?"*

Nothing.

"Ellie? Please, Ellie. Please."

Again, nothing.

"I told him the truth," she said. *"I told the man I met today the truth. Because of you. Because of what you said. And I'm ready to listen to you about our mother. Please."*

"Ughhhhh," came Ellie's voice in her head. *"It's about time."*

Elisabeth found herself letting out a breath she didn't know she was holding. She felt elated—overjoyed.

"Can you come to my flat? I know it's late, but please."

There was nothing, and for a moment, Elisabeth feared she had lost her. But then...

"I suppose. What is the address?"

Eleanor didn't take long to arrive at Elisabeth's flat. She sat at the kitchen table while her sister moved quickly around the little kitchen to make some tea. Within several minutes, a steaming hot cup was in front of each sister as they sat across from each other at the table.

Elisabeth lifted her cup and took a sip, winced at the heat, and then sat the cup down and began.

"I want to apologize," she said. "My age doesn't excuse what I said, but I hope you'll consider that we were teenagers and I, I don't know, I wanted to be loyal to our mother."

"And this morning, too?" Eleanor asked.

Elisabeth sighed. "Ellie, it's hard for me. It still is. But I'm willing to listen now, with an open mind, because I want to get to know Mathias and I don't want our mother ruining it. Please, tell me what she told you."

Eleanor sat in thought before she took a sip of her tea. Elisabeth she wasn't going to tell her, but then she spoke.

"There's a prophecy," Eleanor began, "that a group of Timekeepers would break from those of us who understand these gifts are to be used for good, and not bad. These dark Timekeepers would embrace the gifts of the Forbidden Powers. For whatever reason, there is a rumor amongst the Timekeepers that these powers have never been gained by a Timekeeper. I suppose that stems from the same rumor that there is no original Timekeeping family. Our mother possesses these powers. And she has infiltrated other Timekeepers. She has a circle of individuals who know of the original family, of our family, and they are working to become this dark society of Timekeepers.

"Our mother has these powers. And one of these powers involves being unable to age. Haven't you noticed our mother has never changed our entire lifetime? Sure, her hairstyle has changed, her looks have changed. But she has no wrinkles. She has no grey hair. She is frozen at whatever age she was when she took on these powers.

Elisabeth, she gave up her soul for these powers. It's the reason I left. No one should be able to have that kind of power. I began to question whether any of our powers are good. Even the power of us communicating telepathically. And this prophecy, well, this prophecy states that a woman of the original family would give birth to twin girls. When these girls are brought together, they will bring the world into darkness. It's all about destroying everything as we know it and having these two children lead us all in darkness. It's terrible.

"You and I, we were supposed to be those children. The only reason we're alive right now is because we were twin girls. Like I said, our mother is ageless. I have no idea how old she really is, but I've been secretly communicating with Abigail and we weren't her first pregnancy. She had more than us. They were either boys or single children. She killed all of them. She tried to kill Elijah when we came out, but Aldridge suggested against it. We are alive because she knew she had lost her chance to bear these special children. Now it's our turn. The only way to stop this prophecy from coming true is for both of us to not have children. Now, I can't stop our mother's wrath though, so that is why I left. Please don't think I'm telling you not to have children, but if you do, you'll have to go up against her. And the only other way to stop her, is to kill her. And I can't do that either. No matter how evil she is."

Elisabeth shook her head in disbelief. She believed Eleanor. She truly did. But she just hadn't been expecting everything that she had just been told.

"But if our mother is ageless," Elisabeth began, "can she be killed?"

"From what I gather," Eleanor continued, "she is immortal, but not immune to the effects of actually being killed."

The thought of not having children had never occurred to Elisabeth. She assumed it would always be something she would do.

"I don't know if I cannot have children, Ellie."

Eleanor smiled at her. "I know Lis. And like I said, I'm not telling you not to, I'm just saying that our mother will find a way to make her prophecy come true if you do. Our mother gave up her soul. She'll find a way for one of us to bear children, even if it's in the worst possible of ways."

"Why hasn't she done that already then?" Elisabeth asked her sister. "If she's that evil, then why didn't she, forgive me saying this, have Aldridge impregnate one of us or something."

Eleanor closed her eyes. She knew that was something her sister didn't want to think about, but it still had to be put out on the table. If Elisabeth was truly going to cut ties with her mother, she had to know she was truly evil and there was no good in her.

"My best guess," Eleanor said, "is that she'd rather manipulate us into following her path. If she did any of those horrid things, which again, I wouldn't put past her, she'd lose our trust entirely. And that is one of the components of all of this, including gaining these forbidden powers—gaining the trust of other Timekeepers. It was in her best interests to manipulate, plan, and wait."

"I guess I will meet with her," Elisabeth said, "and tell her I will not communicate with her again."

Eleanor reached out and grabbed Elisabeth's hand. "I wouldn't even do that, Lis. I would just stop talking to her altogether. I might even consider hiding. Dying your hair. I don't know. I wake up, every single day, in fear she'll find me. That something happened to you and now she needs me again. And yes, I know that's selfish, but that woman truly terrifies me. I fear if Elijah hadn't gotten me out when he did, she'd have locked me away. The only thing that keeps me going is knowing that my life is precious to her until her prophecy is fulfilled. Yes, she could kidnap me and do the worst possible things to me, but I know that my life is safe until she gets what she wants. It's sad that I have to cling to that."

Elisabeth nodded and sat there for a moment, thinking everything through. She would need to move. She couldn't stay in this flat. She had to hide. Maybe she could convince Mathias to help her do that. She looked back up at her sister.

"Will you stay in my life?"

Eleanor smiled. "Of course, Lis. We'll have to be secretive, but I will be there for you. I promise."

The two sisters stood up and embraced each other, and in that moment, there was no evil in the world. There was only their love.

CHAPTER TEN

December 1924

The next two years passed by quickly for Elisabeth. She cut off all ties with her mother and eventually moved in with Mathias. Because his father had become ill and upset with Mathias for ending the relationship with Bessie, he went to a spare Headquarters they had for emergencies. It also worked out because he technically couldn't take Elisabeth into the official Headquarters until they were married. Therefore, Elisabeth moved out of her flat in London, leaving no forwarding address in hopes her mother wouldn't find her, and moved in with Mathias at the secret Headquarters located under the Tower of London.

The Headquarters had two entrances. The first was a passageway underneath that one had to swim through the Thames to get to. The second was a door, hidden by the magic of Time, that appeared on the side of the Tower and revealed a hidden staircase leading downward. They were safe here, the two of them. Safe from Mathias' father and his judgmental ways as well as Elisabeth's mother and her prying eyes. Elisabeth never mentioned her mother or anyone in her family to Mathias. He didn't know she had any connections to Timekeepers and that she was in fact an original Timekeeper.

It had been about two to three months into their relationship when Mathias confided in her about his Timekeeping abilities and what he did. Obviously, Elisabeth already knew everything there was to know and more, but she had feigned surprise at his announcement and told him she supported him no matter what.

The two of them were sitting in their living area of the Headquarters, a fire going in the grate in front of them. Elisabeth had curled her body into Mathias'. His arms were wrapped around her and they were looking into each other's eyes.

"I love you," he said. "You have no idea how much I love you."

She smiled at him. "I love you too."

"I've just never felt anything like this," Mathias went on. "For anyone. Only you. I feel like we can be honest with each other about anything. You've made me an entirely different person. I never wanted to go out into the world and explore, but with you, I feel like we could go anywhere and do anything. I want to travel the world with you. Am I sounding insane right now?"

Elisabeth's heart had skipped a beat when he said they could be honest with each other about anything. She hadn't been honest with him. She had been keeping secrets about who she really was, what she really knew, and how dangerous loving her could be for him.

"No," she responded. "You don't sound insane."

He pulled his arm from around her, stood up, and walked across the room to a small end table. He pulled open a drawer, took out a small object, and brought it back to Elisabeth. He knelt down on one knee and clicked open the small box in his hand, revealing a diamond ring.

"It was my mother's," Mathias said. "Elisabeth, will you marry me?"

She hadn't been expecting this. She had no idea why. They had been together for two years now. That was more than enough time for their relationship to progress to this point. But she wasn't sure if it was the right thing to do. Marriage could lead to many things, including children, and she had no idea if she could do that given the prophecy.

"Elisabeth?"

Elisabeth broke herself from her thoughts and looked up at Mathias. He was waiting for an answer. And in that moment, she decided to be selfish.

"Yes," she said.

January 1925

Elisabeth married Mathias on January 31, 1925. It was just the two of them, per Elisabeth's insistence. There was no special dress or flowers, no cake. It was just them along with a priest and a few witnesses at a nearby church. The priest had felt a bit odd marrying the couple, as weddings usually came with many family members and friends, but Mathias and Elisabeth insisted they had none. They were married and a certificate was provided.

That evening, Elisabeth entered Mathias' bedroom for the first time. Even though they had lived together, they had never slept in the same bad or done anything more than kiss.

"I love you," Mathias whispered against her neck as he began to undo her blouse.

"Mathias," Elisabeth said, holding up her hand suddenly, to his chest. "I can't."

Mathias stepped back and looked at her in confusion. "What do you mean?"

"I don't think we can have sexual intercourse," she said.

Mathias rubbed the back of his head in confusion and looked around the room, clearly unsure of what to say. Finally, he looked back at her.

"If you aren't feeling comfortable or ready yet," he said, "I can wait. Just tell me."

Elisabeth shook her head. "It isn't that."

"What is it then?" Mathias asked.

Elisabeth began nervously wringing her fingers and paced about the room. How could she possibly give him an answer without telling him the truth? The wheels in her mind were turning, turning, turning. Finally, she knew what she could do, but she felt horrible for telling the lie. But then, hadn't she been lying all this time anyway?

She turned back to Mathias and looked him in the eye. "I don't want to have children."

Mathias walked over to her and pulled her into his arms.

"You could have told me," he said, kissing her on the forehead.

"I feel horrible," she said, tears coming to her eyes now. These were real tears, even though she had twisted the truth. "I've taken away your ability to have a child of your own. I should have told you before you committed yourself to this relationship."

Mathias continuously rubbed the back of her head, attempting to soothe her.

"It's okay," he said softly. "It wouldn't have mattered to me. There are other ways to start a family, if that's what you want, of course."

She looked back up at him. "Of course. But even then, I just don't know how I can give myself to you completely because of the fear of becoming with child."

"Well," Mathias said, "there are ways. They recently opened a Women's Clinic here in London over the last few years. I believe they have methods of some sort that would prevent you from becoming pregnant. We also, well, we don't have to necessarily go the whole way, if that makes sense."

Elisabeth nodded. She knew what he meant. "Let's try that for tonight, and we can go from there. What do you think?"

Mathias smiled down at her. "I will do only what you're comfortable with."

Mathias did exactly as he said he would that first night, and Elisabeth was grateful. But she also felt guilty for not being able to provide her husband with a child. She just couldn't. She couldn't allow her mother to be able to turn her children into something evil. They would adopt as Mathias had suggested. They would start a family that way. And for now, Elisabeth was content with that.

March 1925

Elisabeth enjoyed the moments she had with Mathias and never wanted them to end. As of now, their plan was working. They had planned to be married for about a year before they started looking into the possibility of adoption.

In the meantime, Elisabeth had visited Eleanor at the orphanage. They continued to strengthen their relationship and life seemed to go on with no problems at all.

That March, Mathias surprised Elisabeth with tickets to the opera. Together, the two of them had a night of fun on the town. However, they both had had a little too much to drink and found themselves embracing each other upon their arrival home. The next morning, when Elisabeth awoke, she knew things had gone a bit different than their previous experiences of being together in that way.

She turned on her side to see Mathias lying next to her. Neither of them had clothes on and while she had had some to drink last night, she still remembered everything they had done. And she remembered her insistence to Mathias that it was alright. They could go all the way. He had asked her several times, and he too had had a few drinks, but she had said it was fine. Her eyes widened and she began to push Mathias lightly to wake him up. He didn't stir.

"Mathias," she said, pushing him again. "Mathias!"

Finally, she pushed him so hard he fell out of the bed and gave a shout.

He stood up, stark naked, his back to her, rubbing the back of his head.

"What in the hell did you do that for?" he asked turning around.

She smiled at the sight of him, completely exposed. He looked down at himself and blushed, covering himself.

"Why are you blushing?" Elisabeth asked. "And why are you covering yourself? I've already seen it."

Mathias looked down and then back up at her. "I have no idea. It's weird getting used to this idea of being married."

He uncovered himself. "It's so nice to be free," he said, doing a twirl.

"Are you still intoxicated from last night?" Elisabeth asked.

"No," he said, jumping back into bed and crawling on top of her. "I'm just glad that I'm here, that I'm married to you, and that I can wake up naked next to you."

She smirked at him. "Well, I'm glad you enjoy being in the nude, but we have a problem. I think I told you to, um, well, you know, last night. To do what we haven't been doing."

His eyes grew wide and she could tell by his expression he remembered now too. He sat up, a serious expression on his face.

"We did," he said. "What are we going to do?"

Elisabeth closed her eyes, trying to think, and then opened them again. "It's fine. If it happens, it happens."

Mathias nodded. "I know you're scared. At least, I'm assuming that's what it is. I'll be with you though, every step of the way."

If only he knew the whole truth. Elisabeth hoped, if she did get pregnant, it wouldn't be twin girls. If it wasn't, they would be fine.

Mathias pulled away and got out of bed. She watched him walk to the door and open it.

"Where are you going?" she asked him.

"To make breakfast," he said.

"Naked?"

He turned back to her, a devilish grin on her face. "We're married, dear. Best get used to it."

Elisabeth picked up the pillow next to her and threw it at him, but he ducked out of the way and left the room.

Elisabeth removed the covers from over her body and looked down toward her belly, placing a hand over it. A normal woman would not be able to tell this early if she was with child, but Elisabeth knew. She was a Timekeeper and had abilities beyond the normal woman. She began to see quick flashes of the future. She saw herself months from now, just before giving birth, feeling her belly with her empath powers, feeling her twin girls inside of her. And then she had flashes of the present, hundreds of miles away, her mother, having the same premonition. It was as if her mother was right in front of her. Slowly, she lifted her face to meet Elisabeth's, her eyes stone cold, and the most evil of smiles painted on her face. Her mother knew and she would be coming. And nothing could stop her. Her mother would find her.

And so it began.

CHAPTER ELEVEN

July 1925

Elisabeth stood in front of the mirror in her sister's bedroom, her blouse slightly raised, her hands on her belly. It was clear as day now to anyone who saw her on the street. She was expecting, and because it was twins, she was larger than most mothers would be. Slowly, Elisabeth moved her hand over her belly and felt the kicking of her daughters. She could see flashes in her mind of her babies in the womb and how peaceful they looked. Would they be able to keep that peace? Or would it all be for nothing?

A knock sounded at the door and Elisabeth lowered her blouse and looked to the door.

"Come in."

The door opened and her sister stepped in, dressed in her habit, and closed the door behind her. In her arms she carried several folders. She smiled, taking a seat on the bed.

Elisabeth looked at the folders. "What are those?"

Eleanor looked at the folders and then back up at her sister. "Potential parents. They all attend St. Patrick's Church in Soho. We work closely with the parish on many matters, adoption being one of them. I brought them for you to review and to pick one. You can also meet them if you'd like."

Elisabeth shook her head. "That can't happen. And why only one? The girls can't be together."

"I know," Eleanor said, "but the orphanage wouldn't allow the twins to be separated if they knew, so we are going to have to pick one family for one child, and then work in secret to find a family for the other. These folders are for you to peruse for the official adoption.

"Also, Sister Margaret is suspicious. We are friends, and I know I can trust her if it comes to it, but I can tell she suspects something. I made the mistake of telling her you were married, so she doesn't understand why you would want to give up your child. I thought about saying it wasn't your husband's, but I feel that might make matters worse, so for now I'm just going to avoid telling her anything. Just be cautious of her presence." Eleanor stood. "I'll leave you to it then."

She made it to the door before Elisabeth spoke up. "Ellie?"

Eleanor turned around.

"Will you stay with me?" Elisabeth asked. "I don't want to do this alone."

Eleanor smiled and nodded. "Sure."

* * *

Elisabeth had always been quick to make a decision and after going through only four, she felt she had picked the best families for one of her daughters. Eleanor kept talking about each families' positive qualities, never letting on to any negatives.

"The Garfields are always helping out at parish functions," she said. "They have two children already, but feel God is calling them to adopt. Oh, and I love the Ainsley's. They are so sweet. They were recently married and have always done lots of work in the community. They plan to have children of their own, but they wanted to help out if there were any children in need."

"I think these are good," Elisabeth said. "I'd like for Sister Margaret to interview them for me. And let me know how it goes. I think it best if you aren't there either."

Eleanor nodded, gathering the folders and standing up. As she did, one of the folders slipped to the floor and the contents of a couple looking to adopt spilled out. Eleanor knelt down and began picking everything up, but Elisabeth stopped her and picked up the picture herself, looking at it carefully. They were an older couple, but they looked so kind, and also so lonely it made her heart skip a beat.

"Who are they?" she asked, looking to Eleanor.

Eleanor smiled at the picture. "Those are the Jordans. Her name is Annette, and I believe his is Dean. They married quite young but were never able to have children."

Elisabeth looked back at the picture and considered it. And then she knew. "I want them. Interview them, but I'm almost certain they should be the ones."

A look of concern passed over Eleanor's face. "Lis, they are older than the rest. What if something were to happen? Your daughter might not have them in her life for as long as she needs them."

"I know," Elisabeth said, "but they deserve a chance. I want them unless something comes up in the interview."

Eleanor nodded. "If you're sure."

"I'm sure," Elisabeth said, handing her the picture.

She walked back over to the mirror as Eleanor left the room and placed her hand over her growing belly again. Slowly, she once again rubbed her hand back and forth.

"I've found one of you a home," she said. "And I know already you'll be very happy there. Now I just need to find one of you the other home and we'll be all set."

Her sister returned after a few moments.

"I let Sister Margaret know," she said as she walked into the room. "She said she'll visit the Jordan home this week and speak with them. Now, we just need to figure out what to do for the other."

"America," Elisabeth said, turning around. "I want the other to be raised in America."

"Lis," Eleanor said, "are you sure?"

Elisabeth nodded vehemently. "Yes. They need to be as far away from each other as they can possibly get. After I have them, I intend to go there anyway. I'll drop her off myself. That way I can spend a little time with one of them."

"What about Mother?" Eleanor asked.

"She won't find me. We are going to do this in secret. She'll never know that I've been working with you and I know now that I'll have to leave Mathias. It's the only way. I will leave him before they are born and he'll be useless to her if she attempts to find him."

Her sister took a deep breath and then nodded. "It's settled then. I'll find someone."

"No," Elisabeth said. "I know just who I can ask."

"Very well," Eleanor said. "But you need to keep me informed. Also, you'll need to find a midwife who can help us with the birth. And we'll need a private location where nobody can find us."

Elisabeth nodded. "I'll start looking."

She moved to the bed, picked up her hat, and placed it on her head. Nowadays she kept her hair up in a tight bun, along with a hat, so as to move discreetly throughout London and avoid her mother's eyes. As she moved to leave, she wondered how she would contact Henry. She couldn't use the Time Line or Mathias' pocket watch, because he could easily discover she had used it and know she was a Timekeeper. She also couldn't use her own because her mother could track her messages to Henry and discover their plan. She knew who she needed.

"Ellie," she said, looking at her sister, "do you still communicate with Elijah?"

"We write to each other," she responded. "Mother doesn't know. He collects his mail in the village. Why?"

"I need him to meet me. Can you arrange a date and location for us to meet?"

Her sister raised her eyebrows in suspicion but didn't question it. "Of course. Tell me when and where."

After giving her sister a date and location, she hugged Eleanor tightly. "Thank you again." She pulled away and smiled, and then walked out of the bedroom and out of the orphanage.

Elisabeth had asked her sister to arrange a meeting with Elijah at St. Patrick's in Soho the following weekend. She arrived early and took a seat in the pew. It was a Saturday, in the middle of the afternoon, and the church was empty except for the few parishioners coming in for the daily reconciliation. As she waited, she continuously moved her hand over her belly. Knowing she would have little time to spend with her children, she wanted to show them as much comfort as she could in the time she had.

A hand touched her shoulder and she almost let out a scream but stopped herself. She turned and saw Elijah behind her. He threw his hands up in surrender.

"Sorry," he whispered. "Didn't mean to frighten you."

He walked around and took a seat next to her in the pew. Before they said anything, the two of them hugged, holding on to each other for as long as possible. They had not seen each other since Elisabeth had left for London, now almost three years ago, and even before then they hadn't been close, rarely speaking or spending time with each other because of Elisabeth's devotion to her mother. She regretted that now.

"I'm sorry," she said quietly when they pulled away from each other. "I shouldn't have let myself be blinded by our mother's abilities."

Elijah shook his head. "You love her. And Eleanor does too. I don't think I ever have or will."

She understood him. While her mother had spent time pretending to be a mother to both her and Eleanor, blinding them from the truth and her true self and unfortunately bringing them to feel love for her, she had never been anything but cruel to Elijah.

"I shouldn't have been the last to see it," Elisabeth said.

He shook his head again. "It's okay."

"Have you seen Eleanor?" she asked.

"We've only written to each other. I planned to stop by the orphanage after our meeting. She wanted all three of us to meet, but I advised her against it. Who knows what our mother would be capable of if the three of us were together. I'm not saying we have any special ability when we're all together, but I just don't want to chance it considering your condition."

He gestured toward her growing belly and she smiled.

"I just wish it didn't have to come to this," she said. And then she explained everything to him. She told him how their mother already knew of the pregnancy and what Elisabeth's plan was for making sure her children were kept safe.

"I plan to leave a note for each family not to try looking for their father," she said, "and that he'll be dead. I know that's the worst lie, but it's the only way. I'm planning to take one of them to America with me, but I'll have someone else take them to the family. I can't risk being identified or having one of them find me later on. But I need your help. I need to contact the American Timekeeper, Henry Jane, and see if he can meet with me here in London. I know I could send him a letter, like Eleanor did for you, but it would take too long and I need him to come to London through the Time Line and meet me privately."

"What do you need me to do?" Elijah asked.

"I need you to go to America and deliver the message for me. Tell him when and where we will meet. And then I need you to disappear."

Elijah shook his head. "I can't leave Abigail. She's practically my mother."

Elisabeth took Elijah's hand and held it to her belly. "I know you love her, but these are your nieces and they need you to do this. It's time to let Abigail go. I love her too, but she's made her choice to stay with our mother. I can't have you going back there now that you know this information."

Elijah looked hurt. "It seems you've tricked me into doing your bidding."

She closed her eyes a moment and then nodded. "I know. And I'm sorry, Elijah. But I need you. I *need* you. I have to protect my children. If this prophecy comes true, what would it matter? What would staying and protecting Abigail matter if years down the line she was going to end up in a world full of darkness and evil? Please, help me."

Elijah took a deep breath and then nodded.

"Tell me exactly what to do," he said.

"Go to the London Headquarters," she said. "You know the way in. Use the Time Line to go to San Francisco and meet with Henry and tell him to meet me here, one week from today, at this same time. Tell him to come alone. He might be written up for unsanctioned travel, but he'll have to endure that. Tell him it's for me. He'll understand. And don't tell him anything about how we know each other. And after that, go and live your life. Don't go back to Ireland."

Elijah stood up. She could tell he still wasn't happy about this. He truly loved Abigail. "Is that it then?"

She nodded and he began to walk away.

"Elijah?"

He turned and looked back at her.

"Thank you," she said. "I hope you'll be able to forgive me someday, but if not, I'll understand. Goodbye."

Her brother didn't say anything and walked away, leaving her alone with her thoughts and daughters once again.

CHAPTER TWELVE

Elijah did as Elisabeth had requested. Exactly one week later, she met Henry Jane in the church. It was the first time they had seen each other in two years. His appearance had changed. His hair, which had once been short, now fell down to his neck, similar to Mathias'. He also sported a fairly impressive beard that looked well-kept.

"Henry," Elisabeth said softly so as not to disturb the peaceful surroundings in the church.

He turned his head and looked up at her from the pew he was sitting in, a smile on his face.

"Elisabeth."

Henry held out his hand. She took it and he guided her into the pew, where she sat next to him.

"How's Thomas?" Elisabeth asked.

It was almost as if Henry's younger self appeared when he thought of his son. A smile erupted on his face.

"Thomas... well, he is my everything. I don't know how I could live without him."

Elisabeth looked at her belly and placed her hand over it.

"I'm beginning to know the feeling," she said. "And Bessie? Did she ever come back?"

Henry shook his head. "I'm afraid not. I've not heard from her since she left Mathias. I've actually met someone, and well, we are due to be married in the summer."

Elisabeth smiled and squeezed Henry's hand. "That's wonderful. I'm happy for you."

"Thank you," Henry said, still beaming. "The man I met with, he said it was urgent. He didn't tell me how you knew each other. And how did he know where to find me? How did he know about..."

She could tell he was struggling to say the words because he was unsure what she knew about the world of Timekeeping.

"It's okay Henry," Elisabeth said, reassuring him. "I know everything. And what I'm going to tell you, I've never told anyone. And it has to stay between us. Is that a promise you can keep?"

He nodded.

Elisabeth shook her head. "But before we get to that, you told me you owed me a favor. Is that still something you can do?"

Henry nodded. "Of course. What do you need?"

"I can't explain everything Henry," Elisabeth said, rubbing her belly, "but I need you to know that this means the world to me. I'm having twins and I'm going to have to give them up. And I know it sounds awful, but they cannot be together. I've already found one of them a home here in London and I was hoping you would be able to do the same for the other in America. They need to be as far away from each other as possible."

A look of grief appeared on Henry's face as Elisabeth explained what she needed him to do. When she finished talking, he looked her squarely in the eye.

"Are you sure this is something you want?"

"Yes."

"But you are giving up your children."

Elisabeth nodded. "I know how it sounds, Henry, but I need you to understand this is for the best. And you'll understand why because of what I'm about to tell you."

And so, for the first time in her life, Elisabeth Callaghan told another person about her family. How they were the original Timekeeping family. How her mother was most likely older than humanly possible. How a prophecy had long ago been predicted and how her mother was dead set on making sure prophecy came to fruition. And finally, how the only way to stop it was to separate her children and keep them out of the Timekeeping world.

When she was done, Elisabeth lowered her head and took a deep breath. It was as if a great burden had finally been shared with someone else. Henry, having seen her distress, pulled her into him and held her.

"I can see how much pain this has caused you," he whispered. "I'm sorry you've had to go through it, but I want you to know I'm here to help."

Elisabeth pulled away, wiping tears.

"Thank you. I suppose everything is settled from here on out. I'll see you sometime in December. I hope you don't get into too much trouble for the unsanctioned travel."

A grin appeared on Henry's face. "I wouldn't worry too much about that. I've made quite a few friends since I've taken over from Bessie's father. But are you sure you are going to be okay between now and then?"

Elisabeth nodded. "I have Mathias, for now. It'll be hard leaving him, and you can't tell him anything."

"Very well," Henry said, standing up. "I'll be heading back there shortly, then. If anything happens, please don't hesitate to contact me."

Henry reached into his pocket and pulled out a pocket watch.

"I may or may not have swiped an extra pocket watch that can be used to communicate with me," he said, handing it out to her. "I know any messages can be seen by those at central Headquarters so be sure you only use it in an emergency and then I'll make up some kind of excuse to come to you."

Elisabeth shook her head. "It's fine. I fear it could make things worse if I have it."

"I insist. It would give me some peace of mind."

Elisabeth looked at it for a moment longer and then finally relented. It could be useful in the end. She let him drop it in her hand and then tucked it into her pocket with the one her mother had given her as a girl. It would also work, but if she used it, her mother could track her. Elisabeth stood and grabbed her handbag.

"Where are you off to?" Henry asked. "I can walk you."

"Oh, no need. I'm off to interview some midwives at a local café.

It'll be boring work."

Henry and Elisabeth bid each other farewell and went their separate ways outside of the church.

The afternoon wore on and on as Elisabeth interviewed various women in hopes of finding a midwife who could successfully deliver her babies. Eleanor had insisted, many times, that she have the babies delivered at the orphanage, with the help of Sister Margaret and the other nuns, but she knew that was too risky. She couldn't risk the orphanage being linked with her children, in fear that her mother would find out.

But the process of interviewing numerous women was tedious, and in each interview, Elisabeth somehow made skin contact with each of the women and saw something within them she didn't like. One woman had an abusive husband. Another had taken to whipping her own children as part of their punishment for being disobedient. While she knew these things couldn't necessarily harm her own children, she couldn't handle the thought of any of them holding her babies.

Finally, when she thought she would have to give up for today, a woman entered the small café, walking back to the corner where Elisabeth sat. She had light brown hair, pulled back into a tight bun, and a soft round face. She was decently dressed, wearing a pink, midi shift dress with a solid, boat neckline. Silver heels clicked on the floor as she approached. She carried with her a small, pink handbag, which she clasped close to her side, and each of her hands were wrapped in pink gloves that matched her dress.

"I hope I'm not being forward," the woman said as she approached, smiling, "but are you whom I should speak to about the midwife position?"

Elisabeth saw the drop of the woman's eyes to her growing belly. She nodded, and they sat down across from each other.

"And what is your name?" Elisabeth asked, looking for a blank sheet she could begin writing on.

"Mildred," the woman responded, "Miss Mildred Waters. I saw the ad you placed in the newspaper."

Nodding, Elisabeth wrote down the name on her paper. "And do you have prior experience with delivering a child?"

"Of course," Mildred said, snapping open the pink handbag and pulling out a folded paper. "Here are my references and previous experiences."

Elisabeth took the paper, wishing she could feel something through the woman's gloves. She opened the paper and perused it. The woman hadn't been lying. She definitely had experience.

"Have you had any difficulties with delivering a child before?" Elisabeth asked.

"No, ma'am," Mildred responded. "I'm pleased to say that all of the babies I've delivered have been healthy and that my references can attest to that."

Nodding again, Elisabeth pretended to continue to peruse the references. She had every intention to contact them later, but she had to think of a way to verify this woman on her own standards. She wondered if it would be odd if she made some excuse to use the lavatory and then come back and accidentally brushed against the woman's arm. But that might look odd. The next best thing would have to be the woman's word. Therefore, she asked a question she had not yet asked one of her applicants.

"How do I know I can trust you?" she asked, looking into the woman's eyes.

The only thing she saw was kindness.

"I would never do anything to hurt a child," Mildred said, reaching out and placing a hand over Elisabeth's. This was something she hadn't been expecting. Something no one else had done.

And in that moment, Elisabeth made the decision to trust Mildred Waters.

CHAPTER THIRTEEN

Four Months Later

Elisabeth looked over at Mathias. She was sitting up in bed, which had been difficult given her current condition, and she was looking down at him, pondering how she had fallen in love with this man. She didn't deserve him. And she especially didn't deserve him after what she was about to do. But there was no way around it. She had fallen directly into her mother's trap. And even though she had had the premonitions, and knew what was going to happen, she hoped it would change. They didn't all come true, right? She hoped maybe it would just be one, and maybe even a boy? Maybe she could keep it then?

As Elisabeth looked at Mathias, sound asleep, one final time, she began to cry. She had taken advantage of this man. Not intentionally. Not cruelly. She had legitimately fallen in love with him. But she had done so many wrongs. She had fulfilled her mother's wishes. She had destroyed a relationship, albeit a poisonous one, but a relationship nonetheless. And here she was, about to give it all up.

She covered her mouth to stifle the sounds of her crying, but it was too late. Mathias had woken up and was peering at her in the darkness.

"Elisabeth?"

She didn't look at him.

Mathias sat up and moved closer to his wife, placing his arm around her neck and pulling her close to him.

"What's wrong? Why are you crying?"

She shook her head. She had to get a hold of herself. She had to go before she went into labor.

"Nothing," she said. "It's just the state I'm in. I get all these weird emotions. Go back to sleep. I promise you, there's nothing to worry about."

"Only if you are sure," Mathias said.

She smiled at him. "I'm sure."

He laid back down and slowly nodded off. Once Elisabeth was sure he was sound asleep, she swung her legs out of the bed and quietly dressed herself. She had placed a small bag with everything she might need in the back of her wardrobe. She grabbed it, took one final look at her husband, and then looked at the framed picture on her nightstand from their wedding day. She reached out, grabbed the frame, and removed the picture. Then she tucked it into her nightgown, put on a coat, and made her way out of the Tower of London Headquarters and into the night.

As much as it pained her, she didn't look back.

* * *

Elisabeth made her way to Mildred's flat in the West End of London. It was dark and gloomy out on the cold December night. She was sure she was drawing attention from the few citizens on the streets. A woman in her condition, walking in London in the wee hours of the morning, was sure to draw the prying eyes of some. But luckily, no one bothered her, and she made it to Mildred's flat in plenty of time.

Mildred had assured Elisabeth she would be available at any time as soon as the contractions started. Elisabeth hoped this was still the case as she knocked on her midwife's door.

A few moments passed before the door opened, revealing Mildred in a night gown, looking groggy.

"Elisabeth," Mildred said. "Is it time? Did you come all this way? Where's your husband?"

Elisabeth shook her head. "He won't be here. But yes, it's time."

Mildred pulled the door open wider and Elisabeth entered.

The flat looked just as it had the last time she had been there. Mildred had set up a bed in her living area for Elisabeth to lay on. Mildred led her to the bed and helped her change into a birthing gown. Elisabeth laid down on the bed and Mildred began moving about to find the necessary items.

Elisabeth emitted a cry of pain.

"Are you alright?" Mildred asked from the kitchen.

"The contractions are getting closer together," Elisabeth responded.

Mildred appeared with a syringe in her hand. "I've got something for the pain if you'd like."

Elisabeth raised an eyebrow. Mildred hadn't mentioned any type of pain medication being used.

"I think I'll go without," she told Mildred.

Mildred shook her head. "Nonsense."

Before Elisabeth could say another word, Mildred was across the room and the needle was plunging into her neck.

Elisabeth felt the effects of the drug immediately. It wasn't stopping the pain. It was causing her to black out.

"Mildred," she said, but her words began to stutter. "W-w-what did you give me?"

Elisabeth blacked out before she heard an answer.

Elisabeth began blinking her eyes. She was waking up. It took her a few moments before she regained complete consciousness, and when she did, she realized several things. First, she was tied to the bed. Second, her contractions were almost unberable; she was close to giving birth. Finally, Mildred and she weren't the only ones in the room; her mother was there as well.

As soon as Elisabeth laid eyes on her mother, she began pulling at the restraints.

Ellie?

She needed this to work. Their connection hadn't worked since they were children, since before they had grown apart. She desperately hoped the bond they had created over the past nine months would work now. She needed it to.

Ellie?

Nothing.

ELLIE! Please, please answer me.

And then:

Elisabeth?

Yes! Ellie, there's something wrong. Our mother is here. They have me pinned down. I can't get away.

Where are you?

I'm in the West End at Mildred's apartment.

I'm coming.

No, wait. Mother can't know about you

What are you going to do then?

Meet me at the Tower Bridge. I'll figure out some way to get out of here.

Okay.

Ellie went silent as Lucinda stepped forward and looked down at her daughter on the birthing table.

"What an unfortunate sight," Lucinda said.

"What's going on?" Elisabeth asked.

"What's going on is you got played little girl," Mildred said.

Lucinda looked at Mildred, fury in her eyes. "Quiet, Bessie."

Bessie?

Elisabeth looked at Mildred. "Who are you?"

Mildred gave Elisabeth a look filled with hatred, stepped forward, and grabbed her by the chin, making sure that Elisabeth was looking directly into her eyes.

"I'm Bessie Watson," she responded. "You probably know me better as Mathias' former finance."

Elisabeth's heart dropped. She had let herself be fooled into a trap. And then the pain came and she let out a scream.

"Enough of this," Lucinda said. "Bessie, get the water. We need to finish this."

"Mother," Elisabeth said through clenched teeth, "please don't hurt my child. Please."

Lucinda slapped her daughter across the face. "You disgust me, you ungrateful little whore. Tell me, is this Mathias' child, or Henry's? And for your sake, you better hope it's twins."

"I've never been unfaithful to Mathias," Elisabeth responded. "And is there no decency in you? Why are you doing this? What does it matter to you that this prophecy be fulfilled?"

"What does it matter to me?" Lucinda responded. "It should matter to all of us. We are all Timekeepers in this room. And for the past thousand years we've had to hide in the shadows and record every little thing these humans do. I'm tired of it. You don't know this about me, darling, but your mother is a lot older than she appears. I've been on this earth for thousands of years thanks to the powers of darkness. And if this prophecy is fulfilled, we can have it all. We will rule them all. We can live forever. Why wouldn't you want that?"

Elisabeth was one step ahead of her mother, but Lucinda couldn't know that, so she shook her head. "No one should want that. It isn't natural."

Lucinda cackled. "Nothing is natural anymore, darling."

And then Abigail appeared. She walked out of the kitchen carrying a pot of water, Bessie in tow behind her.

"Abigail," Elisabeth said, "please, please help me."

Lucinda rolled her eyes. "Say nothing. Put the pot down and go sit until I need you."

Abigail placed the pot down, giving Elisabeth a look of misery as she did, and then disappeared from the room.

And then the pain came again. Within moments, Lucinda was taking charge, and the pain became unbearable.

"Start pushing," Lucinda said.

"I won't," Elisabeth responded. "I won't let you hurt my babies."

A sharp pain spread up Elisabeth's leg as Lucinda stuck a dagger into her thigh.

"Start pushing," Lucinda said, "or I will cut you open."

Elisabeth silently told her children she was sorry. And she pushed.

The next few minutes passed in a blur. There was pain. There was pushing. There was crying. Her own, but also a baby's. And then there was another baby.

"Finally," Lucinda said. "Twin girls." Lucinda turned to Bessie. "You can kill her now."

Elisabeth tried to look over her legs to see her babies before she died, but she couldn't. She was still strapped to the table. But then she heard her mother and Bessie screaming. And then Abigail was at her side, undoing the restraints.

"There isn't much time, miss," Abigail said.

"Thank you," Elisabeth said.

Abigail nodded and pulled Elisabeth across the room to another table where her babies laid. Elisabeth's legs wobbled, however, as soon as she stood up. Blood began to drip down her legs as well. Noticing Elisabeth's discomfort, Abigail found a towel and quickly helped Elisabeth clean herself up a bit. Next, Abigail grabbed a sheet and wrapped each baby up. Elisabeth looked down at Bessie and her mother. They both were lying unconscious on the floor.

"What did you do to them?" she asked.

"Hit them with the frying pan, miss," Abigail responded. "You need to go. Now."

Abigail placed one of the twins in Elisabeth's arms. She was holding the next one when Bessie darted off the floor and lunged at Abigail. Abigail was quick though. She backed away into the kitchen with the baby. Bessie held a knife in her hand and was advancing on Abigail. And then Lucinda began to make sounds on the floor. She was waking up. She wasn't able to use her powers though. She had a nasty cut at the start of her scalp and was clearly still out of it.

"I can handle this," Abigail said. "You need to go."

"No," Elisabeth said.

"GO!"

For the second time that night, Elisabeth quietly said she was sorry to one of her children, and then she turned and ran out of the flat. She began to hear the cries of her child as she ran down the hallway, tears falling from her face. She also heard the horrendous sounds of Abigail and the screams she made. She didn't even want to imagine what Bessie was doing to her.

But she remembered the baby in her arms. The one life she had to protect. The one way she could stop her mother. And even though she had just given birth, even though she had just left one of her children behind, Elisabeth ran as if her life depended on it. But she wasn't running for her. She was running for the newborn baby in her arms. And she knew that God was giving her the energy she needed to get that child to safety.

The moon was bright and lit up the Tower Bridge. Elisabeth clutched her newborn child close to her bosom as she forced herself to push on, regardless of the pain, regardless of the blood loss that she was still enduring from the birth of her children. As she made her way to the bridge, she could see Eleanor looking out over the water, her habit blowing in the night wind, her back to Elisabeth.

"Ellie."

Eleanor turned and took in the sight of Elisabeth and ran forward.

"Lis," Eleanor said.

Eleanor pulled Elisabeth to the side of the bridge and sat her down against the railing, taking the baby from her arms. The baby was sound asleep.

"She's so quiet," Eleanor said, looking down at her newborn niece.

"She wasn't at first," Elisabeth said. "I held her close as I came here and she eventually fell asle—UGH!"

Elisabeth leaned forward in excruciating pain. She needed medical help, she needed to deliver the afterbirth, she knew that.

"We need to get you to a hospital," Eleanor said.

Elisabeth shook her head. "No. Women didn't need hospitals hundreds of years ago. I can get through this. We need to get her to the orphanage."

The color went out of Eleanor's face immediately as she came to the realization that Elisabeth only had one child with her. Eleanor looked down at the child her sister was holding in her arms, almost as if she pitied her.

"I couldn't make it out with both," Elisabeth said, not waiting for Eleanor to say anything. And suddenly she was crying. Tears were pouring from her, uncontrollably. "I left my baby. I left my child, my baby girl, with that woman."

"There was nothing you could do," Eleanor said. "But listen, Lis, I need you to focus right now. Regardless of the fact that you had to leave your other daughter behind, you still have one you need to protect. And I'm sorry to say—" Eleanor looked behind her at the trail of blood that Elisabeth had left in her wake— "you left an easy way to track you."

Elisabeth looked at her daughter in Eleanor's arms. "She'll never be safe. No matter what I do, they'll find her. You need to take her Eleanor. Like we discussed. Bessie, and maybe mother, will come, and they'll do whatever they intend to do."

Eleanor fell to her knees, still cradling the small child. With her free hand, she reached out and took Elisabeth's hand.

"You and I both know that you being dead won't solve anything," Eleanor said. "These are your girls. You know them. They are of you. They need you to be alive, to be watching over them. Or at least one of them. But for their sake, you also need to be dead."

Elisabeth shook her head. "I don't understand what you're saying."

Eleanor closed her eyes for a moment, thinking. She took a deep breath and opened them. "We switch places. We'll switch our clothes. You drop the child off at the orphanage. And then you disappear."

"What?" Elisabeth shook her head. "No. Absolutely not. I will not let you sacrifice yourself for me. They'll kill you."

"It's the only way."

"No. Ellie, no. You don't deserve this. You don't deserve this after how I've treated you."

Eleanor placed her free hand on Elisabeth's cheek and cradled it, tears beginning to fall from her eyes as well.

"Lis," she said, "you know that I've forgiven you. But this is the life that I chose—to be completely selfless, and put others before myself. And it's the only way. You need to be alive for these girls. And for once, we'll have the upper-hand over our mother."

"She'll know it's you," Elisabeth said. "She'll know. And Ellie, you're my sister. I can't let you do this for me. I can't."

"Maybe," Eleanor said, "but you know as well as I do that our mother never does the hard work herself. She might not even come. And that's why you have to let me do this. Because I'm your sister. And that's what sisters do. And these girls need their mother more than their aunt. We need to hurry. Please. *Please.*"

"Ellie, do not act like you aren't going to make it through this."

Ellie shook her head. "There's no time to discuss that. We need to do this, and we need to do it now."

Elisabeth nodded, realizing that Eleanor was right. And quickly, in the darkest corner of the bridge, the sisters switched their outfits, one holding the child while the other changed. Elisabeth, now dressed as a nun, but still bleeding, held her daughter in her arms and hugged her sister, dressed as a woman that had recently given birth in a blood-soaked nightgown.

"I'll come back," Elisabeth said, after she pulled away.

"No," Eleanor said.

"Yes," Elisabeth said. "I'll be careful. But she'll be safe and if no one comes and you're still here, we can go away together."

"Please don't, Lis."

As Elisabeth began to walk away, her daughter in her arms, she continued to nod at her sister.

When she turned away, her sister's voice stopped her.

"Lis."

Elisabeth turned around and saw her sister holding a picture in her hand.

"I just felt this in the pocket of your nightgown," she said, walking up to Elisabeth and placing it in the pocket of her habit. It was the picture that Elisabeth had taken earlier that night, of her and Mathias. "I thought you might want it. Now go and take care of yourself."

Elisabeth began to walk away again but turned back one last time.

"I will come back," she said too Eleanor.

And she turned, leaving Eleanor behind her, not sure if she'd ever see her again.

Elisabeth made her way through Trafalgar Square, everything quiet for the night, on her way to give up her child. She looked down at the sleeping girl in her arms. At her little eyes. Her little nose. Her little fingers. She knew this would only be possible because of one person. Abigail. The only kind of woman that had ever been like a mother to her. The woman that had raised her. And she knew that she would give that woman's name to the child in her arms now. And she hoped that the parents that took her daughter in as their own would honor that.

Elisabeth rounded a corner and there was St. Agnus'. It was sitting at the end of the little street, everything quiet for the evening, still holding that feeling that it was hidden from everything else, tucked away from the real world. Knowing she might still have time, Elisabeth picked up her pace and quickly made her way to the doorsteps of the orphanage. Still holding her child close to her, she began to beat on the door. Over and over and over she beat on the door until a light came on and the door opened.

Sister Margaret, dressed in a nightgown, opened the door. Her face looked puzzled and for a moment Elisabeth feared she would see through the disguise. But she looked down at the baby instead and then looked back up.

"Sister Eleanor," she said, "what's going on? Why did you leave?"

"This is my sister's daughter," Elisabeth said, the lie rolling quickly off her tongue. "I need to leave her."

"You won't be coming back inside?"

Elisabeth shook her head. "I, I just need to leave her. Please, Sister Margaret."

Again, Sister Margaret looked as if she wasn't accepting any of this, but she held out her arms. "We'll need to have you sign some things."

Elisabeth shook her head. "Please, please, just take her. No signatures. No paperwork. Please."

Sister Margaret took a deep breath, but she could tell this woman —this woman who she knew was not Eleanor, but Elisabeth, but wouldn't say—was in trouble. Therefore, she nodded and held out her arms. "I'll take her then."

Elisabeth looked down at her daughter, Abigail, again. This wasn't enough.

"Can I have a moment alone with her?"

Sister Margaret nodded and beckoned for Elisabeth to follow her into the little study next to the door.

"I'll be back in a few minutes," Sister Margaret said. She slid the doors of the study shut and Elisabeth quickly walked over to the small desk at the side of the room, finding pen and paper. She needed to be clear that her daughter could never come looking for her. She could never become involved in this world. She could never find Mathias or attempt to become a Timekeeper. That was part of the curse. If she was never initiated, the curse could never take place. And she knew that once Abigail was initiated, she would be an original Timekeeper, something Mathias had never known about Elisabeth. And the law was different for an original Timekeeper. Elisabeth knew this was the best way, even if it meant she would never know her daughter.

As she held her daughter in one hand, she picked up a paper and pen from Sister Margaret's desk and began to write in the other:

Whoever reads this has taken my daughter in. For that I thank you. I only have two requests that I hope you will honor. First, name her Abigail. It was my mother's name. Second, please tell her when she asks about her biological family (if she ever asks) that she has none. After I am finished writing this, she won't. I will be dead within the next few hours. Her father died not long after I was with child. We had no living relatives. Please care for her as if she were your own biological child. Her birthday is December 8, 1925.

-Her mother.

Her daughter had to think she was dead. Almost as soon as

Elisabeth had folded the paper and clutched it in her hand, the door to the study slid open.

Sister Margaret stood in the doorway. "Are you ready, Sister?"

Elisabeth looked down at her daughter, who had now woken up and was looking at her mother with curiosity, and then lifted her into a hug. After a moment, she kissed her baby on top of her head and then walked briskly across the room and handed her to Sister Margaret. Almost immediately the child began to cry.

Elisabeth took Sister Margaret's hand and placed the crumpled note in it. "For her adoptive parents, from her mother. And please, Sister Margaret, no word of this night to anyone. Simply say she was left on the doorstep of this orphanage and leave it at that. Please? Promise me."

Sister Margaret nodded. "I promise."

And with that, Elisabeth looked at her daughter one last time, and walked out of the study, out the door of the orphanage, and into the night. She had to get back to Eleanor.

As she walked away, she whispered to herself, "Goodbye, my love."

Elisabeth couldn't hear Eleanor. They hadn't communicated since Elisabeth had given birth. Elisabeth was nervous about what this meant. Her heart was beating at a mile a minute. But she knew she couldn't assume the worst. Her telepathic connection with her sister had always been rocky as had their relationship. But it had been so strong earlier tonight. And that was what worried Elisabeth now as she made her way to the Tower Bridge.

She received a few stares from the few people that were walking the streets this late at night. She was after all dressed as a nun and walking through the streets of London in the wee hours of the morning. On top of that, she was walking as though injured because she was injured to an extent. She had not rested since before giving birth. Her body had reacted in fight and flight mode as Abigail had given her the opportunity to get her daughter to safety.

Her mother wasn't even supposed to be there. She had been trying to protect her children from her and had enlisted the help of Mildred to help her. But Mildred had of course turned out to be Mathias' Bessie, and had also been working with her mother. It had all been a trap. And she had fallen for it.

She let herself be comforted by the fact that she had gotten one child out, but her heart pained at the thought that the other would have to grow up with her mother, who she had now barely any love for.

"You can kill her now."

The words that had come out of her mother's mouth after she had her precious twins. The permission she had given Bessie. Elisabeth had meant nothing to her mother. She had only been needed for one thing: to fulfill a prophecy. The prophecy was what her mother loved. It was the only thing she loved in the world.

The pain of a cramp came crashing forth from within her body and she suddenly fell to the ground of the sidewalk she was walking on, letting out a piercing cry into the night. She let the cramp pass and then stood up, knowing the afterbirth needed to be delivered soon. She had to get to her sister.

Elisabeth turned onto Tower Bridge road and made her way to the bridge, but what she saw stopped her in her tracks. Hanging from the Tower Bridge was her sister. Eleanor was completely lifeless. A noose was around her neck, her body glowing in the moonlight.

Elisabeth let out a howling cry and ran to the walkway above the bridge. As soon as she got to the rope she was pulling on it with all her might. It burned her hands as she pulled and then it slipped back through her fingers. She cried out and tried again, but it was no use. She was too weak, too distraught to pull her sister back over.

She let herself fall to the floor of the walkway as the hot, messy tears poured from her eyes. The cry that she let out now was almost inhuman. It was like the cry of an animal. It was the cry of knowing that her sister had died for her. That her sister had sacrificed everything for her. They had both known they might die, but they'd had no inclination that this is what Bessie would do. And she cried even more over the fact that she had treated her sister like dirt for so many years of their lives. It was the fact that her sister didn't deserve this. That Elisabeth didn't deserve to live. But she lived anyway. Elisabeth slammed her hands against the floor of the walkway, over and over and over again. She needed help. She couldn't do this.

And so she took out the pocket watch, given to her months before, and sent a message to the only person she knew that could help her. Their relationship had always been secret. A secret between the two of them. And she knew he would help her and keep the secret of what had happened tonight.

She called Henry.

CHAPTER FOURTEEN

The Tower Bridge loomed over her. And then she saw darkness. But it kept coming back, and then disappearing again. Back again. Gone again.

"Elisabeth!"

Back again. Gone again.

"It's okay."

Back again. Gone again.

"Oh, my god. Please no. Please no."

Back again. Gone again. Was that Henry? Had he come like he said he would?

Someone was moving her body. She felt it. She was being carried. Her eyes opened and she saw stars above her. It was such a starry night. On this night. When her daughters had been born. And her sister had lost her life. But they were gone now. Gone forever? She didn't know.

"Stay with me."

She couldn't open her eyes anymore. It was too difficult. Her eyelids were too heavy.

"Elisabeth! No!"

And then they shut.

She was back in Ireland, standing at the edge of the cliff. The sea was spraying her face with a soft mist. The sun was beginning to slowly creep over the horizon and bring in a new day. And then Abigail was at her side, the wind blowing her hair around her face.

"Is this heaven?" Elisabeth asked.

Abigail looked at her, smiled, and then looked back out at the sea. "I'm not sure."

"What do you mean?"

"It could be heaven, but it could also be some sort of in-between place. Are you ready to leave everything behind, Elisabeth?"

Elisabeth looked away from Abigail and back out at the sea. "I'm not sure. I named her after you, you know."

Abigail nodded. "I know. That was very kind of you, but I don't know if it's something I deserve."

"Of course, you deserve it!"

When Abigail looked back at Elisabeth, her expression was solemn. "I should have done more, to get you, Eleanor, and Elijah away from her. I should have done more."

"What could you have done?" Elisabeth asked. "Seriously? She would have found us. You did the most courageous thing by staying and enduring it all."

A small smile crept onto Abigail's face. "I always thought of you three as my children."

"Are you dead then?" Elisabeth suddenly asked. "Did they—did they kill you?"

Abigail nodded.

"I'm sorry."

"Don't be," Abigail said. "Please. Don't be. But your mission isn't done. I know your goal was to keep your daughters away from your mother, but that hasn't happened. Not entirely. And one day, they are both going to need you. And I know you are going to want to try and find the other one. But you can't. You need to know she is safe for now, but attempting to find her only allows them to know that you survived, and it puts the other one in danger."

Elisabeth nodded. She didn't know what else to say.

"Now go," Abigail said. "Go make me proud."

When Elisabeth finally opened her eyes, after being in a deep sleep for three days, the morning sun was slowly creeping into a room she didn't recognize. At first, her initial reaction was fight and flight, for she thought she was back at Mildred's—no Bessie's—flat and she had never escaped, or they had somehow found her. But then she realized this was an entirely different place.

It appeared to be a young girl's bedroom. There were dolls scattered about the room, a dollhouse in the corner, and a little tea table in another. The door to the room opening broke her concentration.

A girl around the age of ten appeared in the doorway, holding a tray of medical supplies. When the little girl saw Elisabeth awake, she quickly turned around and ran from the room. Had Elisabeth frightened her? Where was she? Who was this little girl? Was Henry here?

And then he was there. Henry walked through the doorway, followed closely by a woman a few years older than Elisabeth. The woman looked familiar, but she couldn't place where she knew her from.

"Henry," Elisabeth said quietly.

He came around the bed and took her hand in his, kneeling next to her.

"It's okay," he said quietly. "Don't try and overexert yourself. This is Dorothy," Henry beckoned to the familiar looking woman, "she's a midwife I had helped out a few years ago when I was still in London. She was the first person I thought to bring you to."

Midwife.

The word made Elisabeth realize how she had known this woman. She had interviewed her all those months ago in the little café. She was the woman who'd been beaten by her husband, and therefore Elisabeth hadn't hired her. And she had hired Mildred—Bessie— instead. Her heart beat faster. Why had she allowed herself to judge this woman because of what she had seen? Henry said he had helped her. Had he helped free her of her husband? Whatever she had seen had probably been a memory that was buried deep in the past. But she couldn't look past it and had hired Bessie instead. And that had led her all the way back here.

Realizing Dorothy and Henry were waiting for her to speak, Elisabeth finally broke herself from her thoughts.

"Thank you, Dorothy," she said. "I truly appreciate it. I should have hired you. I remember you from my midwife interviews."

Dorothy smiled. "No hard feelings, miss. Everything happens for a reason. I'm a true believer in that. I took care of delivering your afterbirth and everything should be fine now except for the occasional after-birth bleeding."

Dorothy had Henry wait outside for a moment while she changed the dressings on where Elisabeth had bled profusely and then helped her change into a new gown. Finally, Henry reentered the room and Elisabeth looked to him.

"You came," Elisabeth said to Henry, who had perched himself at the edge of her bed.

"I said I would," he responded. "I'm sorry this happened to you. I could tell how deeply you wanted to protect your daughters, and I'm sorry it didn't work out that way."

Elisabeth shook her head. "It's fine. Maybe Dorothy's right? Maybe everything happens for a reason?"

Henry looked as if he was unsure about that. She knew that life was still tough for him, even though his son had an actual mother who would help raise him now.

"What exactly happened?" he asked.

She had been dreading this question. How could she possibly tell him it had been Bessie, the mother of his child, who had done this to her? But she did. She told him, and they suffered through it together. She knew she couldn't keep secrets from this man.

A few days later, Elisabeth and Henry sat in front of a fire Dorothy and her daughter had made before going to bed. Elisabeth had finally been able to get up and move around after several days of being bedridden. Henry had told her earlier that day that he would be going back to America tomorrow, and she wanted to spend as much time with him as possible. On the sofa, they sat far apart from each other, but it still felt close to her.

"What do you think you are going to do?" Henry finally asked.

Elisabeth spoke, but continued to watch the fire crackle in the grate.

"I don't know," she said. "I have no money. No transportation. I can't go back to Mathias, not that I intended to. I have to keep him safe and how could I possibly show up, no longer pregnant, with no explanation of what I had done with our children? I truly don't know. My plan had been to use the money I had saved to travel, but I left all of that at Bessie's flat when I fled. I have nothing. Not even my children."

"You have me."

Elisabeth looked at Henry and then everything crumbled. All the walls she had built to protect herself from the world, to keep the secrets from everyone, even Mathias, fell apart. This man knew everything about her. Even the things that no one else knew and would probably never know. Tears poured down her face and Henry moved close to her, pulling her into him.

"It's okay," he said softly against her ear, attempting to comfort her.

A few moments passed while he held her and when they finally pulled apart, Henry looked at her for a moment, and then leaned in and placed his lips on hers. It was just a kiss at first, but then it turned into something passionate. It was as if there had been a small flame between them, but then someone had poured gasoline onto it and now it was a raging fire that couldn't be put out. Within a minute, Henry was on top of her, moving his hands over her body, and then a hand began to move under her shirt and then she realized where they were, what they were doing, and placed a hand on his chest.

"Henry," she said.

And then he was off her and down on the other side of the sofa as if he had just realized that she was vermin and he wanted nothing to do with her. But it was the act they wanted nothing to do with.

"Elisabeth," he said, looking around in fear as if someone was going to walk in on them at any moment, "I'm so sorry."

"It's fine," she said, "I am just as guilty as you are."

"But I initiated it," he said.

"And I let it continue," she countered.

He nodded, continuing to look about the room in fear.

"My wife," he said, "I love her, I, I—"

"You do love her," Elisabeth said. "And I love Mathias. But I think if we are being honest with each other, then we have to admit we have always had feelings for each other."

He nodded, beginning to break down and choke up. "I wanted it to be you and me. That day you walked away with Mathias, I hated myself. I knew there was nothing for Bessie and I, yet I let him take you."

"I didn't feel anything for you then though," Elisabeth said. "I don't mean to hurt you, but my feelings for you have only been very recent, once I realized that I could trust you and tell you things I've never told anyone."

"And my feelings for you dwindled, I thought even went away completely, when I met my wife."

"We'll never speak of this," Elisabeth said. "It was something that happened in the heat of the moment, when we were both vulnerable, and we stopped it before it went any further. This is between us."

Henry nodded. "But Elisabeth, I want to help you. You have to let me help you."

She smiled at him. "You've done enough, and I'm forever grateful."

"At least let me get you to New York," he said. "I will pay your travel, get you away from here and help you find a place to settle down, and then maybe you can find work."

Elisabeth shook her head. "I couldn't ask you to do that."

"Please," Henry said, "I need to do this for you."

Initially, Elisabeth declined, but after further insistence from Henry, she finally relented. The following morning, Henry traveled with Elisabeth to New York City, helping her find a new home, a place where she could start fresh, and then he left her with the promise she would update him on how she was doing. And Elisabeth moved forward, trying for the first time in her life, to put the past behind her.

Part Three

Sacrifice
December 1944

CHAPTER FIFTEEN

Hours had passed since Abigail had curled up in the bedroom provided by her mother and started reading the diary. Thomas didn't interrupt her. He knew she needed this time to herself—this time to finally learn about the mother that had sacrificed everything for her. And it was during this time he too was thinking about his birth mother, because there was something he hadn't told Abigail, something that had happened during the night.

When Abby had been fast asleep beside him, he had broken away to use the bathroom. And it was then that he had overheard all of their parents—Mathias, Elisabeth, and Henry—talking in the kitchen, under the assumption everyone else in the flat was fast asleep. Thomas was no eavesdropper. He respected individual's privacy and expected others to provide him with the same courtesy. But when he heard his name, he couldn't resist.

"Does Abigail know about Thomas' mother?" he had heard

Elisabeth ask.

"Why would she need to know about his mother?" Mathias had responded.

"Mathias," Elisabeth said, "surely you've seen the way they look at each other."

"Are you suggesting they are more than friends?"

"You baffle me," Elisabeth said laughing. "You always miss what's right in front of you."

"Regardless," Mathias said, "why would I say anything? Henry didn't want his son to know, so I respected those wishes and kept that knowledge to myself. But perhaps it is time to tell the boy, Henry."

"It would crush him," Henry said. "He's always been so down on himself. Your girl, well, she's changed him. I've only seen them together for a few days now, but the change is evident. How can I possibly tell Thomas his birth mother is Bessie Watson?"

Thomas had made a beeline straight for the bathroom at that point, carefully opening the door and closing it behind him. He had found himself clutching desperately at the counter in the bathroom, looking at himself in the mirror. That woman, that monster, was his mother? She had given birth to him?

And then he began putting two and two together. He had always been somewhat of a player. Did he get that from her? Was he destined to become insane? Would he hurt Abigail? His father hadn't been lying. The knowledge did crush him. Almost completely.

Thomas had turned and bent over the toilet at that point, throwing up his dinner at the thought of that woman being his mother. He had stayed in there a good long while before returning to the bedroom he shared with Abigail and curling up beside her, attempting to fall asleep and forget about what he had just learned.

And here he stood now, in the living room, looking out the window of Elisabeth's flat, desperately wanting to go into the bedroom and talk to Abigail about it. She would know what to say, surely. But what would she think when he told her his mother had been the one responsible for murdering her aunt? What would she think of him? Would she even want to continue whatever relationship they had growing between them? The questions floated endlessly in his mind as he took a sip from the mug of tea he was holding.

"Alright, Tommy?"

Oliver's hand slapped Thomas on the back and he turned to look at his friend.

"I'm fine."

Oli raised an eyebrow. "You don't seem fine."

"Oli, I—" he hesitated, unsure of what to say, "—I found out something about my birth mother. Something that concerns Abigail."

"Funny you should bring that up," Oliver said. "Back when we were in Cripple Creek she found me up one night looking at old photos. I showed her a picture of your birth mother. She kind of acted like she knew her."

Thomas' insides felt like they were freezing up at Oliver's words. Abigail had seen a picture of his birth mother, and she would've known it was Bessie. She knew. He had seen this picture before, but he didn't know it was Bessie he was looking at. And she had kept it from him. Why would she do that? Was she disgusted by him? He knew that their relationship was still new, but he felt he had a right to know something like this as soon as she found out about it. It almost felt as if she had betrayed him.

"Tommy?"

Oliver's voice broke him from his thoughts and he looked back at his friend.

"Yes?"

"You sure you're okay, buddy?" Oliver asked. "You look like you're going to be sick."

Thomas shook his head. "I'm not okay. I just need to be alone."

He walked to the coatrack by the door, grabbed his coat, and put it on. Then he pulled open the door and walked toward the stairs. He needed to get some air.

The diary sat open on my lap for a long while after I finished reading it. I had gone into a bit of a trance, staring out ahead of me, thinking of the words my mother had written on these pages. I knew everything there was to know about her life until my birth, and even a little after. The letters from Henry would serve as her telling me what she did after my birth—what she had been doing for the last nineteen years. But I didn't want to read them. I knew now I would put them away and let her tell me the stories herself. When this was all over— when we could finally be together—we would spend hours talking about all of the things I had missed about her life.

And I would tell her about mine. About my parents, Annette and Dean, and how I missed them every single day—how I wished, so desperately, I could go back and save them from the war that took them from me. I would tell my mother all of these things about my life, and then we could be together. Mathias and Elisabeth would never replace my parents, but they would be there for me, and I knew my parents would want that.

Knock. Knock. Knock.

I looked up. "Come in."

The door opened and Oliver stood in the doorway, and the look on his face told me something had gone terribly wrong. I was out of the bed and across the room before he could say anything, the diary left open behind me.

"Oliver? What's wrong?"

Oliver blinked a couple of times, as if he wasn't sure where he was, before he finally spoke.

"I didn't realize that Thomas' mother was that—that woman."

Bessie.

"How did you know?" I asked him.

"Thomas overheard Henry and your parents talking about it last night," he said.

My heart began racing. That was why Thomas had looked off this morning. He had found out the truth about his birth mother.

"Where is he?" I asked, pushing past Oliver and into the hallway.

When I walked out into the living room, it was empty. No trace of Thomas. Alma walked out of her bedroom and looked between Oliver and me.

"Is everything okay?"

I shook my head and looked back at Oliver.

"What happened?"

"Abigail," he said, "I'm so sorry. I didn't know Thomas didn't know you had looked at that picture of his birth mother. He knows you've been keeping it from him."

My heart came to a complete stop. He had found out I had kept this from him. I had kept something so personal from him, so as not to hurt him, but ended up making it worse anyway. I looked back at Oliver.

"Where did he go? Oliver?"

Oliver shook his head. "He just said he needed to be alone."

You're so vulnerable, Melanie said inside my head. *And now Thomas is mine.*

"No," I said to the room. "She has him."

I ran across the room, grabbed my coat from the rack, and pulled open the door.

"Abby!" I heard Oliver and Alma say behind me, but I ignored them.

Thomas needed me.

The events of San Francisco were following them. Thomas could feel the drop in temperature that had taken place overnight as he walked the streets of Paris, his hands tucked in his pockets. But the cold was, surprisingly, not bothering him. His mind was elsewhere. It was on the fact that Abigail had kept this from him. It was on the fact that his father had kept this from him. That is his mother was a woman who had murdered a person, maybe even more than one person for all he knew.

Thomas stood on the Pont Alexandre III, looking at the Eiffel Tower. He hadn't imagined he would be in Paris with the world potentially ending. He knew the elite few who would survive this would create a world that wasn't worth living in. And to him, that was the end of the world.

"Thomas."

He turned and saw Abigail walking up behind him, her hands also tucked away in the pockets of her coat, which was a slightly different shade of blue then what he had remembered it. He looked away and back at the Eiffel Tower.

"Did Oliver tell you?"

"Yes."

She was behind him now, placing her hand on his shoulder, forcing him to turn his head and look down at her, into her eyes. And he could tell now it wasn't her.

"Melanie."

A smile crept onto Melanie's lips. A smile that didn't fit the face of the girl he loved.

"Perhaps your relationship with my sister is a bit more serious than I previously thought?"

"I love her," Thomas said. "Do you honestly think I wouldn't be able to recognize the girl I love?"

Melanie cocked her head to the side. "Love is such an archaic idea. I don't really believe in it."

"You should," Thomas said, looking around now to investigate his surroundings and assess the gravity of the situation he had found himself in.

"There's nowhere to go," Melanie said softly.

And she wasn't lying. From one end of the bridge came Lucinda, in no particular hurry, and from the other end, came Headrick. He was sure Ian was close by.

"What do you want?" Thomas asked.

"You," Melanie responded. "Abigail needs a little push to give herself up. And for you, she will."

Thomas shook his head. "You don't understand her at all. She sacrificed her fiancé, knowing the world wouldn't survive if she didn't. She would do the same thing for me. She's strong and doesn't need me to get through this."

"Perhaps," Melanie said, "but the world isn't at stake here. She'll come up with a plan to get you back and to save humanity at the same time. She'll come for you."

"Thomas!"

Thomas turned at the sound of Abigail's voice. She was approaching from the end of the bridge where Headrick stood. But then Melanie held her hand up next to his face and everything went dark.

Thomas was on the bridge as I approached, but so was Melanie. And Headrick was blocking the way, her back to me.

"Thomas!" I shouted.

He turned his head to look at me and then Melanie used her powers to knock him on unconscious. He slumped to the ground at her feet as Lucinda walked past, making her way to my end of the bridge.

"More people are going to be hurt, Abigail," she said as she approached. "This can all end if you come with me now. We will let Thomas go."

"Come with us."

It was Ian. He was behind her. She turned to see him approaching with Aldridge.

"Stay away from me," I said.

"It really doesn't matter now, does it?" Lucinda asked. "You're outnumbered. Are you really going to resist?"

And then there was a loud, booming sound and the earth began to shake. It was an earthquake and the bridge began to vibrate, causing everyone to lose balance.

"Forgive me," I whispered, turning on my heel and surprising Ian by pushing him down.

"Stop her!" Lucinda shouted.

But they couldn't. I was running and, before long, I was off the bridge. It separated from my end, creating a gap between the bridge and the street. They couldn't get to me, but I kept running and running and running back toward my mother's apartment. We had to leave. Now.

The only thing going through my mind as I ran was the fact that I had failed again. I had failed Thomas. And I was out of time, with no way to contact my mother. The world was closing in on me, and I wasn't ready for it. And then, because I was vulnerable, Melanie broke through once again.

You have twenty-four hours, she said in my mind. *After that, he's dead.*

CHAPTER SIXTEEN

Once I had made it back to my mother's apartment, the temperature had dropped tremendously and it had begun to snow. We were running out of time. And now I only had twenty-four hours until Thomas was dead. This had to end now. And my mother needed to help me end it.

"Abby," Oliver, Alma, and Perrine said together as I entered the flat, closing the door behind me.

"They have him," I said. "They have Thomas. And they are giving me twenty-four hours to come to them."

"But we don't know where the Headquarters is," Alma said. "How can we stop this and turn back time? There's no way for us to get in."

"Lucinda needs me there to finish all of this," I said. "That much I know. We need to use that to my advantage."

"But your mother," Oliver said, "we have no idea where she is. We need her."

"I know, but she'll know. We have some sort of connection that I've yet to understand, but I know she'll know it's time."

Alma and Oliver looked at each other, unsure whether any of this was going to work. Perrine stood in the background looking confused about it all. I knew it was all still new to her. Finally, Alma looked back at me.

"What's your plan then?"

I looked to Perrine. "I need you to turn me in."

Perrine's eyes went wide. "I can't do that."

"Yes, you can," I said. "I know we don't know each other very well, but you chose our side when you helped Thomas. And I'm thankful for that. But they don't know that yet. If you bring me in to the Paris Headquarters, then Headrick can take me to Lucinda. And from there, well, hopefully I can stall long enough to give my mother time to get there."

For a moment, I thought she was going to refuse again, but she nodded.

I looked to all of them now.

"We don't have much time," I said. "I'm going to get some rest and we will go tomorrow. The three of you will need to be prepared to follow us, wherever we go. Perrine will have to be observant after she turns me in. I'm sure Headrick will use the Time Line to take me where we need to go in Ireland. And from there, things will move quickly."

Perrine looked to Alma and Oliver.

"I can sneak you both in," she said. "We may need to doctor your appearance a bit since they know you're with us and you're wanted, but it should be pretty simple. Timekeepers have always been a bit too trusting anyway."

I couldn't even begin to express how true that statement was. I let the three of them stay in the living room to hash out the details and made my way to the bedroom Thomas and I had stayed in. I curled up in the bed and pulled the pillow he had slept on close to me, letting his lingering scent engulf my senses. I would get him back. I had to keep holding on to that.

"It's the only way."

Elisabeth looked from Mathias to Henry. After telling them the entire truth, she felt as if she were the worst person on the planet. Perhaps it was true. Her life had been a series of ups and downs in which she had focused only on herself. The only thing she had ever cared about, had shown complete selflessness for, had been her children. And what she was asking of the men in front of her now, she couldn't even fathom how it would be forgivable.

Mathias put his face in his hands. Henry looked around the room as if he might be ill.

"I'm so sorry," Elisabeth said. "The fact that I'm asking this of both of you, after everything I've put you both through, is unforgivable. But I'm thinking of our children and their future now. And this is the only way I can make sure they have the future they truly deserve."

"I'll do it."

Elisabeth looked at Henry. He had spoken clearly and his eyes were dead-set on her now.

"I never stopped loving you, Elisabeth."

She closed her eyes and nodded at Henry's comments. The evening Mathias had returned to her, she'd let him know the truth. That she had fallen in love with another man, but that she still loved him as fiercely as the day they married. And he had held her and accepted that, and for the first time in years, they had shared a bed together.

Henry looked over at Mathias.

"I'm sorry, I didn't mean to change the topic of this conversation."

Mathias put his hand on Henry's shoulder.

"It's fine. She's told me and it's alright. And you know I will always love you Elisabeth, and I will do this. For you. For our children. For Henry's son."

Elisabeth smiled and then fell forward on the table and began to convulse. The two men looked at each other, concern drawn on their faces, but they didn't interfere. They knew she was having a premonition. A few moments passed, and finally Elisabeth's eyes opened,/ and she sat back up.

"What is it?" Henry asked. "What did you see?"

She looked back and forth again between the two of them.

"It's almost time," she said.

Elisabeth placed both of her hands, palms up, on the table. The men she loved placed their hands in hers and they sat like that, the three of them together, for quite a while.

Sleeping was difficult without Thomas by my side. I tossed and turned throughout the night, occasionally waking up from a nightmare, only to turn to Thomas for comfort and find the other side of the bed empty. How had I come to care for him so completely and then proceed to hide the truth from him? I knew I kept it secret because I cared for him, because I didn't want to see him get hurt, but I had still hurt him in the process. And there was nothing I could do to fix it. He was gone.

But I was going to get him back. I had to hang on to that thought. I was going to get him back.

There was a creaking sound as the door to the bedroom opened and closed.

"Abby?" Alma's voice came out of the darkness.

"Yes?"

"I'm sorry if I woke you," Alma said, coming to my side of the bed and falling to her knees. I could make her out in the moonlight pouring in through the bedroom window.

"It's fine, I wasn't really sleeping at all."

I could tell that Alma was visibly nervous. She was playing with her hands and rocking back and forth on the balls of her feet. I reached around her and clicked on the bedside lamp.

"Is everything okay?"

She looked away for a moment and then looked back, shaking her head.

"Tomorrow, or well, today now," she began, "well, it could change everything. This is about Oliver and, well, he hasn't expressed any interest in me."

I knew that a smile was growing on my face.

"I'm fairly certain he's interested."

"Then why won't he tell me?" she asked.

"Maybe he's afraid?" I suggested. "There is a lot going on right now."

Alma nodded, looking down. "I know there is. I just want to be with him."

Reaching out, I touched the tip of Alma's chin and she looked back up at me.

"Tell him," I told her. "Tell him how you feel. Remember, you said tomorrow could change everything. Maybe it's now or never? Tell him."

"You think so?"

"I know so," I responded. "Tell him."

Alma extended her arms and pulled me into an embrace. We held each other, in that moment, as if tomorrow would never come. But the truth was, it already had.

Alma went back to her room and I fell back asleep. This time, I was able to stay asleep, and it was actually peaceful. Talking to her had given me hope. Hope that everything would turn out okay. Hope that I would fix everything. Hope that nothing would go wrong.

A *chirp, chirp, chirp* from outside my bedroom window woke me in the morning. When I opened my eyes, I looked over to see a robin perched on the windowsill. And a memory came back to me, from all those months ago, back when I was in London with Bridget. Back before everything about my life, except for the fact that I was a Timekeeper, had changed forever.

She had said that the robin lives each day with no worries and no fears. She had said I was clearly going through many things in my life right now and shouldn't be afraid. And here I was, almost a year later, living in a world without her, without my parents, without Phillip. And now without Thomas.

But the strange thing about it all was I wasn't afraid. I was no longer afraid of the darkness. I was no longer afraid of what would happen. Because I knew that I had to fix this. That I would fix this or I would die trying. And so, I climbed out of the bed and walked over to the window, looking at the robin still perched on the windowsill.

"Whatever happens, happens," I said to the robin. "And I won't be afraid."

CHAPTER SEVENTEEN

The four of us made our way to the Paris Headquarters early that morning. Perrine had done quite the job on making Alma and Oliver look completely different using some makeup as well as a few changes to their hairstyles. And my heart had lit up when I walked into the kitchen finding the two of them holding hands. Upon seeing me, they had quickly pulled away from each other, their faces growing red. I simply smiled and went about my business.

Now as we walked through the streets of Paris, Alma and Oliver hovering somewhere behind us so as not to draw attention, my thoughts were focused on the task ahead. I had to get into the original Headquarters and turn back time. Getting in wouldn't be the problem. It would be getting around Lucinda and whatever she had planned. And I hoped my mother was ready to do whatever she needed to do. Because now was the time.

As we walked toward the Eiffel Tower, the only thing going

through my mind was the fact that this was it. This was the end. And I hoped, I prayed, that it would end in my favor.

"Of course, they would put the Headquarters under the Eiffel Tower," I said to Perrine as we drew closer.

She looked back at me and smiled. "I forget you're still new to all of this. It's actually the other way around. Non-Timekeepers put the Eiffel Tower on top of the Headquarters."

I nodded. I should have remembered this. Mathias had explained it to me once when I inquired about the London Headquarters and its location under Big Ben.

"Are you afraid?" Perrine asked as we drew closer.

"No. I've spent so long being afraid that I can't be anymore. Now I'm just angry. And determined to end all of this."

"I can understand wanting it to be over, but make sure you're careful. Also, once we get closer, I will have to take you in as if you're a prisoner."

"I understand," I said.

The temperature was continuing to drop. I hugged myself. We were walking across the grass now, approaching the tower.

"We have to take the elevator when no one else is on it," Perrine said.

I nodded and when we approached the ground floor elevator, we waited until we would be the only ones on board, plus Oliver and Alma. They stood off to the side, appearing as if they had no connection with us at all. The doors closed and Perrine took a pocket watch from around her neck and tapped it on the elevator panel. All of the buttons lit up simultaneously and then the elevator began to descend into darkness. And then there was light as we descended into the Paris Headquarters. It was everywhere. Lights dangled from the ceilings in strips, twinkling. Balls of light were attached to long cords that fell from the ceiling. In the middle of the room stood a giant clock, the hands removed to represent that time was forever—it never ended.

"We take the name City of Lights seriously here at the Paris Headquarters," Perrine said, a smile on her face.

"I think it's beautiful. Is Headrick stationed here then?"

"She technically still has her old office here," Perrine responded. "But most days she's at the Central Headquarters."

"I see."

"But now I have to take you prisoner," Perrine said. "Are you ready?"

I looked at her and nodded. She gripped my arm as if she was using force to bring me in and then when the elevator came to a stop, the doors opening, she led me out and up to a desk not too far away where a receptionist sat.

"I need to see Angela Headrick immediately," Perrine said to the receptionist. "Tell her I have Abigail Jordan in custody."

Guards came and led Perrine and I to a set of stairs. They led us further and further down until we came to a single door. A plaque on the door read *Councilor Angela Headrick*. The guard pushed open the door and I was led into a spacious, round office. Lining the walls were various portraits of events in history. And in the center of the room was a large mahogany desk. Lucinda sat behind it and standing near her was Headrick.

"Thank you, gentlemen," Headrick said to the guards. "You are dismissed."

Headrick looked over to Perrine. "You've proven yourself to be quite dependent Ms. Naudé. I assume you have other business to attend to, but if you'd like to stay, you are most welcome. We could always use some additional assistance."

"I'd like to stay if that's alright, ma'am," Perrine said.

"Very well."

Once the guards left the room, Lucinda stood and walked over to me. Her heels clicked against the floor menacingly as she circled me. I had no idea what she was doing or if she was looking for something. And then she looked at Headrick and spoke.

"Will you excuse us, Angela?"

Headrick nodded and beckoned for Perrine to follow her out of her office, closing the door behind her.

Lucinda turned back to me and then walked back to the front of the desk, perching herself on the tip of it, crossing her arms, and looking at me.

"You and I are similar, Abigail."

"I'm nothing like you."

She smiled. "Oh, on the contrary, you are. You see we've both felt like outsiders at one point or another. You used to believe you were insane because you heard those whispers growing up. You were afraid to tell anyone about it. If I remember correctly, Melanie even told me friend of yours, Bridget, thought you should seek help for it. Melanie's been listening to you for a long time, you see. I too have felt the shame of having to hide my true self from the world. And with this prophecy, with what it entails, we will no longer have to hide. We will rise above everyone else as the dominant and more superior race."

"Rise above who?" I asked. "Everyone's going to die given the Time Line resetting itself."

Lucinda grinned again. "People will die, yes, but people will live too. Humans have survived an Ice Age before. Believe me I know. I was there."

"How old are you?" I asked her.

Lucinda shrugged. "You lose track after a while. But believe me Abigail, I've been around long enough to know that humans are never going to change. Unless we reset the scales and show our true selves from the beginning, they will always live in fear of us should we expose ourselves. They will always fight against us and attempt to destroy us. It's ironic, given the fact they can't live without us."

"I'm done listening to you. I won't help you."

And then she smiled that smile again. That smile that made my skin crawl.

She walked over to me and leaned in close, whispering into my ear.

"I don't need your help," she said. "I already have you. And that will suffice. Forgive me for trying to make things a little better for you."

She stood up straight and called out, "Angela."

The door to the office opened and Headrick peeked in. "Yes, ma'am?"

"Have Ms. Naudé take her to a cell. Prepare for travel. We will depart in the morning."

Headrick nodded and Perrine gripped my arm again and took me away. As she did, I hoped against all hope I'd be able to see Thomas.

Perrine led me to the Time Line of the Paris Headquarters.

"The prison for Timekeepers is at Central Headquarters," she said as we descended another level.

"Will Thomas be there?" I asked.

"He should be."

"And what about Oliver and Alma?"

Perrine glanced about as we walked through the corridors, most likely checking to make sure that we were alone.

"They'll have to hide away here tonight and follow us in the morning," she finally said. "I'll keep them informed."

It was then I realized we had ended up at the end of a corridor, a large door from floor to ceiling rising in front of me. Perrine took out her pocket watch and placed it in a circular indention in the door. The oak door lit up and then began to ascend, slowly sliding up into the ceiling, revealing the Time Line behind it.

"It's always fascinated me how every Headquarters is different," I said to her. "The London Headquarters always seemed so simple. And then the San Francisco Headquarters felt grand and made the world seem so much larger. This place makes it feel like a different world entirely."

Perrine looked over and smiled. "I suppose it just shows how different we all are underneath. No one person is the same. Something Lucinda doesn't seem to grasp."

"She's lived for thousands of years," I confided in Perrine. "She's been alive all this time. She's seen it all. How am I possibly going to stop her?"

Perrine squeezed my arm. It wasn't painful, but reassuring.

"You've made it this far Abigail Jordan," she said. "Now isn't the time to start doubting yourself."

I looked ahead at the Time Line. "I won't be afraid."

I wasn't necessarily speaking to her, or to anyone. Maybe I was speaking to myself? I didn't know. But I had to remind myself of this morning. Of the robin. And how I couldn't be afraid of what was to come. How I had to let whatever would happen, happen.

"I can't go with you, I'm afraid," Perrine said.

"I figured as much."

"Are you ready?"

Looking back at the Time Line, I hesitated for a moment, and then nodded.

"Whatever happens, happens," I said, and I took a step forward.

CHAPTER EIGHTEEN

Upon arriving at the Central Headquarters, I was immediately taken down to the prison. When they mentioned the word "prison," I had assumed it would look like a normal prison, but that was far from the truth. The Timekeeper's Prison was made up of a single, wide-open room with large circles in various spots. These circles represented clocks.

The guard who had escorted me down to the prison took me to an open circle. And as he took out his pocket watch and laid it into an indent in the floor outside of the circle, I realized Thomas was in the circle next to mine. His back was to me, which was why I hadn't seen him upon entering the room, and he appeared to be sleeping. The entire room was rather odd and I didn't quite understand it until the guard placed me inside the circle and walked away. Curious, I reached up and out and found myself trapped by an invisible wall.

Throughout the room, other circles were filled with people, about ten in all. Most of them were asleep, but some of them stared off at the wall, completely out of touch with reality. To me it felt worse than a normal prison. There were no beds. Were we expected to sleep on the cold, stone floor? Did they feed us? Did they allow us to use a bathroom? None of these questions had been answered for me. And while I knew it would be rude to those around me, I knew I needed to talk to Thomas. And so I said his name. But he didn't respond.

"Thomas," I said louder.

Looking around me, I was surprised to see no one paying attention to my raised voice. So, I screamed, but nobody flinched. They couldn't hear me. Whatever this barrier did, one of its powers was keeping out all sound. Or, not keeping it out, but keeping it in.

Knowing Thomas would wake up at some point, I let myself fall back against the invisible barrier and sit on the floor. I couldn't sleep though. He could wake up at any time and I needed to be ready when he did. Hugging my knees to my chest, I waited for Thomas.

The strangest thing about being in a circular prison that most likely represented a clock was that I had no idea how much time had passed and no way of keeping track. I might have been sitting there for hours for all I knew. But it was also possible only a short amount of time had passed. Finally, Thomas began to stir, stretching his arms out in front of him. He then stood up and walked around his circle, stretching his legs. I stood up so he could see me more clearly, and when he looked up and saw me staring at him, his face went through several different expressions.

At first, he seemed angry, but the anger was quickly wiped away and replaced with concern. He looked at me with so much concern I knew in that moment we would always come back to each other, even after the worst of our arguments.

He moved his lips.

Can you read them? he asked.

I nodded and then used my lips as well.

I might not be the best interpreter though.

He smiled, holding up his hand to the invisible wall. I did the same and imagined that I could feel the palm of his hand against mine, our fingers curling together, even though we were in different circles.

I'm sorry I kept the truth from you, I said. *I just didn't want you to get hurt.*

He nodded in understanding, absentmindedly tracing his index finger over the wall.

From now on, he said, *you need to know you can tell me anything. Anything. I will.*

I yawned, confirming my suspicion that I had been there for quite some time. I needed rest.

Get some sleep, Thomas lipped to me. *I'll be here when you wake up.*

I love you, I said to him through the glass.

It was the first time that I had said it to him. He had said to me at a time when I thought my world would never be the same. We had said it about each other to others. But I had never said it to him. And his face changed then. It turned into something that expressed how much he wanted to bring down the barriers between us.

I love you, too, he said.

And with that, I let myself slide back against the wall and slowly fall asleep.

* * *

"Wake up."

I heard the words and I knew the voice. Ian. I couldn't fathom the idea of looking at him, so I kept my eyes shut. And then came a kick that made me cry out in pain.

"Don't you fucking touch her!" I heard Thomas shout.

And then I heard a groan of pain from Thomas and my eyes flashed open, finding him out of his cell and on the floor in pain, a guard standing next to him.

"I don't recall asking you to speak," Ian said, looking down at Thomas.

Thomas looked up at Ian with daggers in his eyes but didn't say anything more. Ian looked back at me watching the two of them and smiled.

"Hello, Abby."

I shook my head at him. "You've lost the right to call me that. You've lost the right to even use my name."

Ian shrugged. "Very well."

He stepped forward and grabbed my arm, wrenching me up off the floor and causing me to groan in pain again.

And then everything else happened in a split second. Thomas broke free of the guard's restraint and was barreling across the room. Ian didn't even have time to be surprised before Thomas threw himself into him, slamming him against the wall and punching him square in the face. Ian slumped to the floor and the guards ran across the room and threw Thomas to the ground.

Clicks of heels against the stone floor pulled everyone's attention away from Ian. We looked over to see Lucinda entering the room, already dressed for travel in a trench coat.

"My, my," she said looking around the room. "Ian, don't you think it is at all possible for you to complete the simplest of tasks without a revolution breaking out?"

She looked down at Ian on the floor, but he was unconscious.

"Pity," Lucinda muttered. "Someone take care of that and make sure he's brought along. It's time to go."

Thomas and I were led from the room, following Lucinda into the long corridor beyond. Outside of the prison, Melanie, Headrick, and Aldridge stood waiting for us. As always, Melanie looked identical to me, except for her expression. It was cold, dark, and calculated. She appeared as if she would always be one step ahead of everyone around her.

We walked along the corridor until we came to the pools of water that represented the Central Headquarter's Time Line. Lucinda stood in front of the water and held her hand out over it. She didn't even require a pocket watch to control her powers.

"After you," Lucinda said to me, stepping away from the pool of water.

The guard pushed me forward and together we stepped into the pool of water, leaving the Central Headquarters behind us.

Dingle, Ireland

We stood on a beach, the waves crashing against the jagged rocks of the shore. A cliff stood on the side to us. And then Lucinda appeared, followed by everyone else. Ian came last, awake now, and continuing to throw murderous looks at Thomas. A black eye would be developing where Thomas had punched him and a feeling of satisfaction rose in my chest.

Lucinda brushed past us, walking to the side of the cliff, and pulling a dagger out of her coat. She rolled up her sleeve and made a cut in her arm. And then she smeared her blood onto the rocks of the cliff and an entrance appeared out of nowhere. She turned around and gestured for us all to enter. This was it. This was the original Headquarters. This is where I could fix all of this. This was the end.

The guard restraining me pushed forward and I followed Melanie and the others. Lucinda entered behind us. And another feeling of satisfaction rose when I realized she wasn't closing the entrance behind her, leaving it open so that Elisabeth would be able to enter as well.

We descended into a circular room with archways over hallways that led in different directions. In the middle of the room was an altar. It stood on top of a giant clock. As they always were in the Timekeeping world, the hands of the clock were missing. I looked to all of the hallways and wondered which one would take me where I needed to go in order to reverse Time and get us back to where we needed to be.

Lucinda walked ahead of us and removed her trench coat.

"Let's not waste any time here," she said. She looked to Aldridge and Headrick. "Place them on the altar."

Aldridge stepped forward and took me from the guard, guiding me over to the altar and beckoning for me to lie down. Headrick did the same with Melanie.

I looked around me before lying down. This was happening too fast. Where was she?

"Who?"

My body froze at Melanie's voice.

"What?" I asked.

"You said, 'where is she?'"

I didn't respond. Melanie looked at me suspiciously and then over at Lucinda who was pulling out an old, withered-looking bound book.

"She's hiding something," Melanie said.

"It doesn't matter," Lucinda said.

She was flipping through the pages of the book, trying to find something.

"But she is."

Lucinda looked up at Melanie. "Quiet!"

Melanie looked down in shame and in that moment I felt sorry for her. Regardless of all the horrible things my sister had probably done in her lifetime, I felt sorry for her.

Lucinda walked over and reached out to grip Melanie's chin.

"Nothing matters anymore," she said, almost motherly. "Now lie down."

Melanie did as she was told and Lucinda looked over to me. Taking one last glance at the entrance and everyone around me, I did the same. Whatever would happen would happen. I would wait a moment longer, and then I would fight if I had to. I lied down, waiting for something to happen.

"This is the end," Lucinda said, reading from her book, "but it is also the beginning. A new age is upon us. And the two of you will lead us into it."

The only thing going through my mind was *please come. Please. Please come.*

CHAPTER NINETEEN

Lucinda stood over me on the altar, her hands hovering over me. And then the same power Bessie had used that night on the Tower Bridge emitted from her palms. It was the energy of Time but there was a darkness to it. My eyes closed and I began to see all of the terrible things people did to each other throughout Time. War. Destruction. Death. The images flashed before my eyes.

I had never felt like this in my entire life. The feeling was darkness. I felt as if nothing good existed in the world. I saw myself conquering the Timekeepers. I saw myself leading us into a new age where we did not have to hide away protecting the people. We could begin a new reign. One in which we had total control over what happened in the world. We could use Time to our advantage, rather than stand by and let it rip us apart as it showed us what we cannot change. There is no such thing as sacrifice.

Yes, there is.

A voice from within me spoke resiliently. It was my own voice. My voice that was being weakened by this darkness. It needed to be conquered. There could be no room in me for love or kindness. There could be only darkness. There is no sacrifice; there is only what we can take from the world. Instead of sacrifice, you must eliminate the threat. We must rid the earth of those who will stand in our way. They will only cause us to lose sight of the true goal. Total control.

I was still there. But I could feel myself losing. This new me, this darker me, was trying to take over. They say there is evil inside of us all. Is that true? When I think of evil, I think of the darkest parts of the world. I think of Hell. Could there really be something like that in us? I suppose there had to be. Otherwise, why would we sin? Why would we lie and steal? Why would we pretend to be something we're not? I know now there is darkness in us all. But we must choose to live outside of the darkness.

This love, this peace—it needs to go away. I cannot let it prevail.

"Mother."

And it all stops. The thoughts, the images, the darkness—it all leaves me.

"Mother."

Lucinda's concentration ceased upon hearing her daughter's voice. It couldn't be. After all this time, why would Eleanor show up here? But when she turned around, she saw it wasn't Eleanor, but Elisabeth along with a number of other Timekeepers following in her wake. She was consumed with rage.

"You!" she spat.

"Hello, mother," Elisabeth said, walking into her home as if she

213

had any right to be here. Elisabeth cocked her head to the side as she considered Lucinda. "It seems, for perhaps the first time in your life, you are the one that has been tricked. Eleanor and I switched places that night, but your little servant couldn't be bothered to tell the difference. I suppose that's what you get for sending someone else to do your dirty work. But you've always done that, haven't you mother?"

A guttural, animalistic sound erupted from within Lucinda and she brought up her palms, throwing her powers at her daughter. The power to freeze a person where they stood, frozen in Time, along with the power to age. She had to destroy Elisabeth once and for all.

Elisabeth held up own palms, resisting her mother's power and moving closer.

"It won't," she said, "WORK on me. Did you honestly think I wouldn't spend as much time as possible practicing for this moment? Training myself to be concentrated by power if such a moment ever came about."

"Lucinda," Headrick called, "what do we do?"

"Protect the girls," Lucinda shouted.

"How long can you possibly last, mother?" Elisabeth asked.

"As long as you can, my dear," Lucinda answered.

"I wish you could've been better," Elisabeth said. "Didn't you have some humanity at all? At one point in your life?"

Lucinda looked like she might reveal something, but she held on. "You will not beat me! I am forever. I am the TIMEKEEPER."

Elisabeth continued to hold, producing the barrier stopping her mother's powers. She knew her mother wouldn't approach her for fear that someone might attempt to kill her. She knew she was safe. And she knew her daughters would be safe if she could only hold on.

"Enough of this!" Lucinda shouted over the chaos. "You cannot win, Elisabeth."

Elisabeth ignored her mother's insistence that she would lose and kept holding strong.

My eyes opened. Whatever Lucinda had been trying to do had stopped completely. Elisabeth—my mother—had come. She had come just as she said she would. I had thought she'd left me again, but it had been for good reason. She needed this moment. This moment where her mother did not have the upper hand. Where *we* had the upper hand.

Swinging my legs off of the altar, I leaned down and picked up the dagger Lucinda had dropped. I would end this. She had done what we needed her to do, and now it was up to me to stop this before the prophecy came to fruition.

I looked around the room. Mathias, Henry, Perrine, Alma, and Oliver had entered alongside my mother and were attempting to hold off the others with whatever protective powers my mother had given them. It was as if they were being protected by some magical shield that Elisabeth was setting off, but the shield only went so far. It didn't extend to her and Thomas on the other side of the room. Melanie was still out cold on the table. No one stood in my way. Lucinda was vulnerable.

Taking my chance, I marched toward Lucinda's back, clutching the dagger in my hand.

And then I was being pushed to the ground by someone from behind, my head pressed to the concrete, and the dagger was wrestled from my grip.

"I will not let you hurt her," Melanie hissed in my ear.

I wasn't going to let her stop me now. Bringing up my knee, I hit her as hard as I could in the stomach. She rolled off me, screaming in pain. I grabbed the dagger and began to stand, but Melanie's hand clutched my ankle, bringing me back down.

"Let go of me," I screamed, attempting to kick her away from me.

"I will not," she said, "LET YOU HURT HER."

I began to worry I might not get her to let go, that I might fail, when Thomas appeared behind Melanie and pulled her off of me.

"Let go of me," she shrieked.

"Abby, go," Thomas said.

But Thomas didn't have Elisabeth's protection. Melanie quickly took her opportunity and brought her wrist up in the air to use her powers. Thomas bellowed over with pain, falling to the floor, clutching at his chest.

"Thomas!"

I began to run toward him, but he held up his hand.

"Leave me."

"Are you going to let him die, Abigail? Come on, dear sister of mine? Are you just going to stand there?"

It was almost as if Lucinda's power had been used on me and I was completely frozen in time. I could save Thomas now, but then what would happen? Would we still make it through? This is what Melanie wanted. I looked at Thomas on the ground, the pain overtaking his face. There were tears building up in his eyes now. Tears from what? From the pain? From the idea of dying?

"How much longer can you hold on, Elisabeth?" I heard Lucinda shouting from behind me.

Turning my head, I looked at my mother, in battle with her own mother, and I could see she was weakening. At the end of it all, even after having had the upper hand, Lucinda was stronger. She had been going strong for thousands of years. And she had to be stopped.

I looked back at Thomas. Melanie still had her hold on him, and she wasn't worried about me. Like my grandmother, she trusted I would make the opposite decision of what I was about to make. The decision I had made once before in my life. The sacrifice I had taken. They didn't understand me, and they never would.

If I didn't do this now, I was going to lose absolute control and break down. He was the last person I truly had. And Lucinda thought if I lost him, I would go her way. The way of darkness. But she was wrong.

I shook my head at Thomas.

"I'm sorry," I said quietly. I knew he could read my lips even if he couldn't hear it.

"I know," he mouthed back. "It's okay."

His face tightened even more from the pain. I knew then she was somehow using her power to manipulate his heart. She was killing him from the inside. And it made it even worse as he slowly uttered the next three words.

"I—love—you. Forever."

Before the light could leave his eyes for good, I turned on the spot and marched toward Lucinda. Melanie turned her head.

"NO!" she shouted. "LUCINDA!"

As soon as I reached her, Lucinda whirled on her feet and was facing me. Her icy blue eyes, eyes that had seen this world change over thousands of years, stared back at me as I plunged the tip of the dagger into her heart.

She looked down at the dagger and then back up at me. And she smiled. It was the strangest thing. I looked into her eyes and it was almost as if something that hadn't been there, something that had been gone for so many years, returned to them.

Elisabeth walked up, still somewhat weakened, and stood by my side. She looked at Lucinda.

"Goodbye, mother."

Lucinda dropped to her knees, looking up at the ceiling as she died. And as she did, a single tear rolled from her eye.

"I'm sorry," she said, looking up at the ceiling one last time, and then falling forward on her chest, dead, her eyes still open.

I had no idea if the words were to me, or to some long-lost part of her humanity that had been forgotten. But it didn't matter. All of the years she had cheated death began to catch up with her. Her smooth, soft skin began to shrivel and wrinkle. The pure gold hair she sported began to grey and then turn a pearly white, before crinkling up and falling out completely. And then my grandmother became bone, and then she became dust. And then it was all over.

Elisabeth looked over at me.

"It's all over," she said. "We beat them. And you were so strong, holding off against her, until I got here."

I smiled, but then remembered.

"Thomas," I said, turning and going back to where I had left him to die. As I did, I saw Melanie. She was curled up next to Thomas, hugging her legs to herself, and shaking.

"I killed him," she was saying, almost as if she had not intended to do just that. "I stopped his heart."

Henry ran up and knelt down next to his son, putting his hands on his chest and beginning compressions.

"What's he doing?" I asked, looking at Oliver, who had also appeared.

"He's trying to resuscitate him," Oliver responded. "To restart his heart. There might be enough time to bring him back. Henry learned it during the war."

Nodding, I looked back at Thomas' lifeless body on the ground.

Please, please come back to me. Please God, let him come back to me. Let me have this one person. *PLEASE.*

Henry kept doing the compressions, occasionally breathing air into Thomas' mouth. We all stood there, completely silent, watching Henry attempt to revive his only son—his only child. Melanie was still curled up nearby, unable to come to terms with what she had just done, and I assumed, everything she had done before this.

Henry was almost beating on Thomas now, and tears were running down my face. Finally, Oliver walked over to Henry, fell to his knees next to him, and attempted to pull Henry away from his son.

"Henry," he said calmly. "He's gone."

"No," Henry said quietly. And then he shouted again, this time like an animal in agony: loud, guttural, anguished. "NO!"

He let himself fall into Oliver, who held him.

And then there was an audible intake of breath. Then a cough. And then Thomas' eyes opened and, even though he was still in pain, he managed to look over at his father and past Henry—to me.

"Thank you," Henry said, looking up at the ceiling and then falling next to Thomas. "Thank you, God."

Thomas looked up at his father, a cheeky grin on his face. "'S matter pops? You look like you've seen a ghost."

Henry laughed and pulled his son into him. Mathias came over to Elisabeth and I and put his arms around us, pulling all three of us together. Oliver stepped away from Henry and Thomas and embraced Alma.

A few moments passed, and then Henry let go of his son.

"Abby?" Thomas asked.

I broke away from my parents and walked over to him, falling to my knees in front of him.

"I'm sorry," I said.

"You needed to do it," he said. "Otherwise, the you I know wouldn't be here. And this world is not worth living in if I can't have that version of you."

He leaned up and kissed me. After that, we stayed still, our lips barely touching, our foreheads against each other.

"I love you," I said.

"And I love you," he said.

I let myself pull away and look at Melanie. We had to figure out what to do next. Perrine had control of Ian, Alderidge, and Headrick.

She had managed to find some rope to tie them up with. They had weakened considerably after their powers had ceased to exist.

Standing upright, I walked over toward Melanie, Elisabeth rejoining me at my side.

"The bit of humanity my mother stole from her is returning," Elisabeth said. "I think she is beginning to realize what she has done. What she has been coerced into doing."

I walked over to Melanie and leaned down in front of her.

"Melanie?"

She looked up at me. "Stay away from me."

"It's okay," I said, reaching out, but she moved further away from me.

"You don't know the things that I've done," she said. "The things that I've done to people. I can't."

I heard Elisabeth approaching me and she leaned down as well.

"Melanie?" she said. "I'm your mother. And I'm so sorry I abandoned you."

"You didn't have a choice though, did you?" She looked up at Elisabeth. "I know what they put you through."

And then her eyes lit up as if she remembered something.

"You have to reverse time," she said, looking from me and then to Elisabeth. "And I know it takes a sacrifice of three. Let me do it. Let me do something right for once."

"No," Elisabeth said, looking at me and then back at Melanie. "It's your time now, you can't let yourself feel guilty for the things Lucinda made you do."

"I always will," Melanie said. "I always will, and there's nothing you can do to take that feeling away from me. Who else is going to do it? It has to be a willing sacrifice. And I am willing."

"What is she talking about?" I asked.

Elisabeth sat back on the ground, sighing. "The part I didn't want to tell you about. In order to reverse the Time Line, to alter it so that you never did what you did in San Francisco, there has to be a sacrifice of three, willing to give their lives to save everyone else."

I shook my head. "No, there has to be another way."

"There isn't," she said. "There never is, is there? And your father, Henry, and I are going to do it."

"No," I said. "I won't let you."

"Dad," Thomas said, "is this true?"

I realized Thomas had walked up to us now and had overheard.

"It is, son," Henry said. "We need to restore order and let our children live their lives."

"Let me do it," Melanie said, grabbing Elisabeth's hands. "You shouldn't have to. *Please.*"

Elisabeth shook her head, smiling. "Absolutely not. It was selfish of me, but after I gave you up, I had nothing to do but live my life. And I did. I traveled to different places, made friends with so many different people. I could have come to find you, but I didn't."

"Because you were trying to keep the prophecy from coming true," Melanie said. "Who knows what they would have done otherwise?"

"Perhaps," Elisabeth said, "but now I have the chance to give you the life I always wanted for you. And you're going to have it."

Elisabeth stood up, brushing off the dirt on her dress, and turning to address me.

"After you found me, I consulted with Mathias and Henry about how to reverse the Time Line. They volunteered without a second thought."

"But this is my mistake," I said, standing up as well. "I have to be the one to fix it."

My mother stepped forward and pulled me into her, holding me tightly. And then she pulled away, placing a kiss on my forehead as she did.

"I am your mother," she said, "and it is my job to help you fix your mistakes. At the end of the day, this all comes back on me. And there is nothing you can do to change that. You two have each other now, and you'll have a bond that meant so much to me and my sister Eleanor. And Abigail, you have Thomas. Melanie, now is your time to meet someone of your own, to love and to care for, and to feel things you haven't been able to until now. This is the way it has to be. And that is all we are going to say on the subject."

She turned to look at the others.

"Oliver, Alma, and Perrine," she said, "I am going to have you use the Time Line here, after we have reversed time, to take Headrick and Ian back to the Central Headquarters. The stories my mother passed to me in my training state that Time will rewrite itself over the past month. The three of us will go back and change what Abigail did. It'll still be today when all is said and done, but Abigail won't have done what she did. Everyone that died as a result of what happened in San Francisco will be alive again, but everyone who died for any other reason, as in the case of Lucinda, will remain dead. Unfortunately, that includes your friend, Bridget."

She looked at me and smiled, but it was one of sadness. But I understood.

"Only the people in this room will remember what happened," she went on. "All other people, including Timekeepers, will only have knowledge of the way in which Time rewrites the past month. While all of you will remember what happened here today, you will also have this knowledge of how Time changes things. I'm sure, for example, it will come up with a different way for how Bridget died. Furthermore, it should also come up with a reason for why Headrick and Ian will be prosecuted. Finally, it will most likely remove all mention of the Forbidden Powers, now that the prophecy can no longer be met. Now, Oliver, Alma, and Perrine, if you'll wait here, I will take the others with me."

And with that, she led us further down into the Headquarters until we reached a wall. Elisabeth took the pocket watch I had returned to her and placed it into a whole in the wall. The wall slowly slid back to reveal an underground cavern. It was like we were standing on the sand of an indoor beach. The water stretched out for miles before me. But we were still inside, in a cavern. My mother, I now realized, wore the white dress I had always seen in the visions she had sent me, only her hair was much shorter now. She turned around to look at the five of us: myself, my father, Melanie, Henry, and Thomas.

"This is Time."

Her voice was firm. She extended her arm out before her to indicate the vast lake.

"Just as time is endless, so is the water."

I stepped forward and walked to the edge of the water.

"This is how you turn back Time?"

I stepped a bit closer, my foot almost touching the water, but my mother grabbed my arm.

"Once you go, there is no coming back."

She held open her arms to both Melanie and I. "Come here."

We both went to her and let ourselves fall in them. Being in my birth mother's arms like this for the first time made me feel complete. Her arms held me tightly and I felt a wetness on my cheek and realized she was crying. And my sister, my sister was with me, and she no longer had the darkness in her.

"I know you will not understand this," Elisabeth whispered, "but some day you will. Children make mistakes, and sometimes it is up to the parent to fix them. Yes, eventually the child must mature and learn to fix their own mistakes, but that day is not today. I will fix this for the both of you. And then you will be on your own in this world, but I'll always be with you in here." She touched one hand to each of our hearts. "My beautiful girls, together at last."

"I feel like I've let you down." The words came out uneven in my tears.

She smiled at me and shook her head.

"I couldn't be more proud of the woman you've become," she said. "We are all human. We all make mistakes. I made the mistake of trusting the wrong people, and I've paid dearly for it. I gave up a life with you and your sister to ensure you would be safe. I never dreamed it would end up like this, but I have the chance to make sure you are safe again, and if I have to give up my life to do that, I will. The three of us will."

"Remember, only those Timekeepers who were here today will have memory of the events that took place," she continued. "No one else will remember a thing. And I believe it is best they do not. The story of an original Timekeeper will continue to be a myth and nothing more, as it is meant to be. As original Timekeepers, both of you have more power than anyone else, but be wise with what you do with it. After I am gone, you will have the powers I have. But if you do not want to use them, that is okay. There are enough Timekeepers in this world that can enforce the laws. They do not necessarily need us anymore, and that was the intention when we passed along our powers centuries ago. All three of our deaths will somehow be written into the minds of those we knew that weren't here today, but the rest of you will know the truth. It is up to you what you wish to do. If you, Melanie, and Thomas no longer wish to be Timekeepers, then I'm sure they will find a suitable replacement.

"I am so very sorry your father and I were not present more in your lives, girls," she said. "And Abigail, I am so very sorry you were forced to grow up in a war that claimed the lives of those you love. The only thing I can say to that is that it is life. You have done so well with it and you will continue to do well with it. I love you both so much."

There was no more talking, only tears, and some laughter as Thomas and his father shared some memories. We all held our loved ones closely for as long as we could, until finally, it was time to say goodbye. Together, my mother, along with both of the men she loved in life, stepped into the water. They walked further and further in, until they were gone.

CHAPTER TWENTY

May 8, 1945

"This is a solemn but a glorious hour," President Truman said over the radio. "I only wish Franklin D. Roosevelt had lived to witness this day. General Eisenhower informs me the forces of Germany have surrendered to the United Nations. The flags of freedom fly over all Europe."

Thomas had told me it was coming, but I wanted to hear it for myself. Freedom. For all of the people Hitler had imprisoned. Justice, for all of the people he had murdered—my parents and Phillip included. Tears fell down my cheeks as I listened to the rest of the address, and, once it was concluded, I flipped the switch off.

The door to the apartment opened and Thomas came in.

"Did you hear?" he asked.

I nodded. He came over and sat down next to me on the couch, pulling me into him.

"How did your meeting go?" I asked.

"Well, Alma will be taking my place as Head of the American Headquarters."

"That's wonderful."

"Yes, and now it's time for us to do our thing."

He kissed me on the forehead and then went to make dinner.

A lot had changed since my mother, Mathias, and Henry had reversed what I'd done. The Council found Ian and Headrick guilty of crimes to bring down the Council. Both of them had tried to tell the truth about the original family, but no one believed them. Aldridge, as it turned out, was not a Timekeeper in anyway, and after the events at the original Headquarters, he no longer remembered anything that had to do with the Timekeepers and went about his life, even though he didn't deserve to. Melanie and I had spent several months together, working through her pain as well as my own, until she felt ready to go out into the world. She was currently living in London, where she'd always wanted to go, and writing me every few weeks. She worked the odd job here and there to support herself while she took classes. She was hoping to be a nurse. Thomas resigned from Timekeeping once we returned to San Francisco, but stayed on to train the new Timekeeper, which as I just found out, would be Alma. Timekeeping was not what he wanted to do and he knew it was the right decision to make. It was also not what I wanted to do. Thomas and I would both live the rest of our lives with these strange powers, and we would have to prepare our children for them and let them make the decisions of how they wanted to proceed with them, but for us, that was okay.

With the changed events, Bridget had been struck by a vehicle the day she left me at the San Francisco Headquarters to go to class. I knew there had been a funeral for her in this new Time Line, but Thomas, Melanie, Alma, and Oliver helped me with a private memorial for her upon our return to San Francisco. I was able to finally mourn her death properly, as well as the deaths of my mother, Mathias, and Henry, and move on.

As for the original Headquarters, now that Lucinda was dead, along with all of her children, it belonged to Melanie and me. We chose to close it off entirely. Only select people knew about it now, and that was the way it was meant to be.

Thomas began living with me at the Chambord building and later that evening at dinner, he stopped eating, and took my hand.

"I love you," he said.

He looked at me for a moment, considering me.

"I mean, I know you may still feel something for Phillip and—"

I cut him off.

"I love you," I said, "and I'll always love Phillip, but I love you just as much."

The worry on his face melted away. In less than a minute he was out of his chair and lifted me into his arms. Our lips made contact and moved against each other. He carried me to his room and we fell into the bed. He kissed my neck and my forehead.

Later on that night, I was lying next to him. He was sleeping quietly and had me pulled close to his chest. As I looked up at the ceiling, thinking about what had happened today, the end of the war in Europe, I spoke softly.

"Mum, papa," I said, "and Phillip, I know you are up there. I love you so much, and today you received justice. I know that will never bring you back, but I want you to know I will always hold you close to me. And while you'll always be there for me, I know I have to move on now. Completely. So I guess, well, I guess it's goodbye for now. Until we see each other again."

And with that, I closed my eyes, letting Thomas hold me close to him, and drifted off to sleep.

EPILOGUE

Four Years Later

Sleep had me in its arms. A deep, deep sleep. But something was pulling me out of it. The tip of a finger was tracing my eyebrows, over and over and over again. A nose, the edge of it, was rubbing against mine. Finally, I allowed myself to be pulled from sleep's arms. Opening my eyes, I saw Elisabeth, my daughter. She was smiling and prodding at me to wake up.

"Mama," she said, lightly tapping the edge of my nose, "time to wake up."

"It is," I said, smiling. I did my best to push myself up, but considering I was seven months with child, it was proving to be a difficult feat.

"What are you doing?" Thomas asked, walking into the room wearing an apron over his pajamas. "I told you to call me."

He lifted Elisabeth off the bed and helped me up.

"I still try to do some things on my own," I argued.

"Elisabeth Kate," Thomas said, attempting to chide but failing miserably, "I told you, mommy needs extra sleep."

"I want to play," Elisabeth argued.

Thomas laughed and picked her up, balancing her on his shoulders. Elisabeth had recently turned two. She had come along nine mere months after Thomas and I married. Upon marrying, we'd moved to Ireland. We were nowhere near the original Headquarters, but still close enough to keep an eye on the place. Thomas and I helped manage a library in a small village, and not to far from there we'd had a cottage built on the sea, and this was the home we had made for Elisabeth Annette Kate Jane, named after Thomas's true mother as well as both of my mothers, for the sacrifices they made for us all. Our plan was to use all of the names of those we loved in some way or another. I had no idea if I was going to have a boy or a girl with our next child, but I planned on calling him Henry Dean Phillip Jane if he was a boy. We figured our children would simply have to get used to having multiple names.

"It's a nice morning," Thomas said. "I thought I could bring the food out by the cliffs and we could have a picnic."

I smiled and nodded. "That sounds nice. I'll get dressed and take the blanket out."

Thomas took Elisabeth back to the kitchen and I began getting ready for the day. As I got closer to having my second child, I considered what it meant to make sacrifices for your children. I had never understood why my mother wanted to make the sacrifice she did for Melanie and me until I held my baby girl for the first time.

And then it had all made sense. And I was forever grateful to both of my mothers and all they had done for me, along with both of my fathers.

I quickly bathed, found the white dress that reminded me of my birth mother, and put it on. And then I was out, walking toward the cliffs, with the picnic blanket in hand. Once at the cliff's edge, I laid it down, smoothing it out, and then walked a bit closer to the edge, looking out over the sea. The sun was halfway in the sky and the colors were beautiful.

The waves rattled against the seashore as I looked out at the ocean. Seagulls flew through the air. The whiteness of their feathers caught my eye. Suddenly, a light mist of sea waves sprayed me and I smiled as it touched my cheeks. I was getting the oddest sense of de ja vu. And then it hit me. Years ago, I had had a premonition when Phillip was still alive. It had involved another man and I was afraid—afraid because Phillip wasn't with me. But he had assured me he wanted me to move on if something ever happened, and I had.

And I knew now who that man coming up behind me was. It was Thomas.

"Abby," he said, placing his hand on the small of my back.

I turned my head around to face his and we kissed. Elisabeth was at his side and we all stood together as a family.

"Daddy," Elisabeth said, "I want to see it all."

Thomas leaned down and picked Elisabeth up again, once again placing her on his shoulders. And then he stood behind me, placing his arms around my waist and placing one hand on my belly. And we were a family. I let myself fall back into his embrace, his closeness.

The three of us stood together, as one family, as the rest of the sun crept over the horizon. In that moment, there were no whispers, there was no war, no death, and we had enough time.

THE END

Acknowledgments

The elation I felt after completing my first book was something I'd never felt before. But the elation I feel after completing a trilogy of books, well that's something else entirely.

I wrote the first draft of *The Timekeeper's Daughter* in early 2013, during my college years, on an old laptop and on many pieces of paper in many different notebooks. There were many times when, instead of listening to my professor lecture about British literature, I was tucked away in the back of the classroom, scribbling down ideas (a.k.a. "taking notes") about Abigail Jordan and the adventures she would go on in the world of Timekeeping. Oh, spoilers ahead in case you're some strange creature that reads the acknowledgements of the final book in a trilogy before anything else. You've been warned.

Abigail's story first came to me when I imagined a girl, running to save the man she loved, but for some reason, she couldn't. And I asked myself: why can't she save him? What's stopping her? And from there, I built a story.

The deaths Abigail faced in the first book were always there. They weren't thrown in last minute for shock value. Bridget was always going to die in book two. And Abigail was always going to meet and fall in love with Thomas Jane. The story was always there. It was just getting it into words that was often the frustrating, yet equally fun, part of the process.

I'd like to thank Andrea Berthot for editing my book as always. Her attention to detail as well as her own experiences with the creative writing process is something I've always admired.

Thank you to Alexander von Ness for the amazing cover design as always. You've truly translated Abigail's story, in each of the three books, into a unique visual. I truly appreciate that!

And thank you to my family, friends, and all those that have read Abigail's story from beginning to end. In the end, the reader matters the most, and I hope I've delivered a story that made you think, imagine, and most importantly, served as an escape for you, if only for a little while.

CPSIA information can be obtained
at www.ICGtesting.com
Printed in the USA
LVHW112038220520
656320LV00007B/36/J